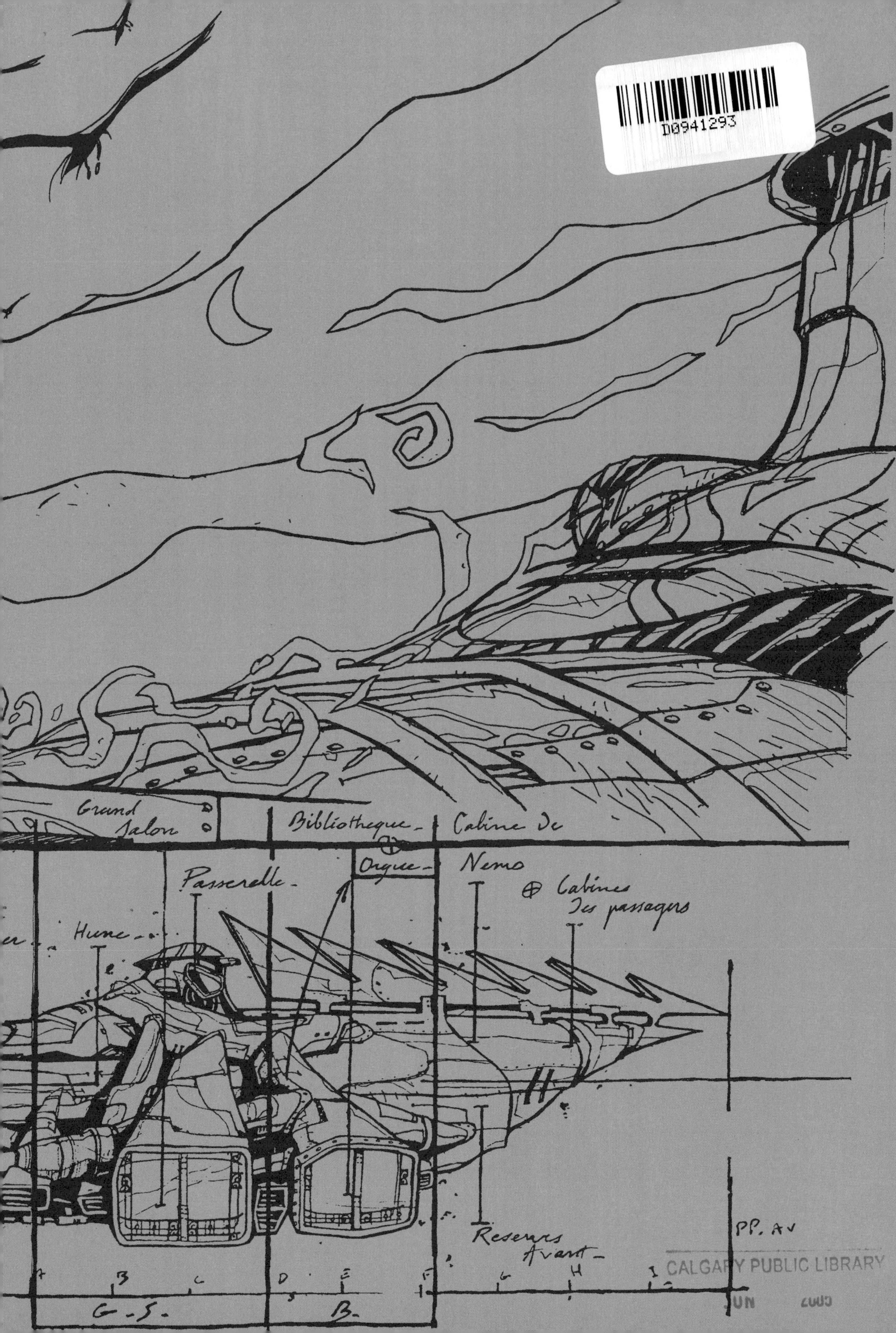
Grand Salon
Bibliotheque
Cabine De Nemo
Orgue
Passerelle
Cabines Des passagers
Hune
Reserves Avant
PP. AV
A
B
C
D
E
F
G
H
I
G. S.
B.

Library of Congress Cataloging-in-Publication Data

Rivière, François, 1949–
[Voyage sous les eaux. English]
Voyage into the deep: the saga of Jules Verne and Captain Nemo / François Rivière, Serge Micheli, Sebastien Ferran.
p. cm.
ISBN 0-8109-4830-3
I. Micheli, Serge. II. Ferran, Sâebastien. III. Verne, Jules,
1828–1905. Vingt mille lieues sous les mers. IV. Title.

PQ2678.I8737V6913 2004
843'.914—dc22
2003015193

Illustrations and original text copyright © 2002 EP Éditions, 7 rue d'Assas, 75006 Paris
English translation text copyright © 2004 Harry N. Abrams, Inc.

Published in 2004 by Harry N. Abrams, Incorporated, New York.
All rights reserved. No part of the contents of this book may be reproduced
without the written permission of the publisher.

Printed and bound in China
10 9 8 7 6 5 4 3 2 1

Harry N. Abrams, Inc.
100 Fifth Avenue
New York, NY 10011
www.abramsbooks.com

Abrams is a subsidiary of
LA MARTINIÈRE
G R O U P E

VOYAGE INTO THE DEEP

The Saga of Jules Verne and Captain Nemo

Text by
FRANÇOIS RIVIÈRE
Design by
SERGE MICHELI
Color by
SÉBASTIEN FERRAN

HARRY N. ABRAMS, INC., PUBLISHERS

CHAPTER ONE

THE AQUA MIKAN

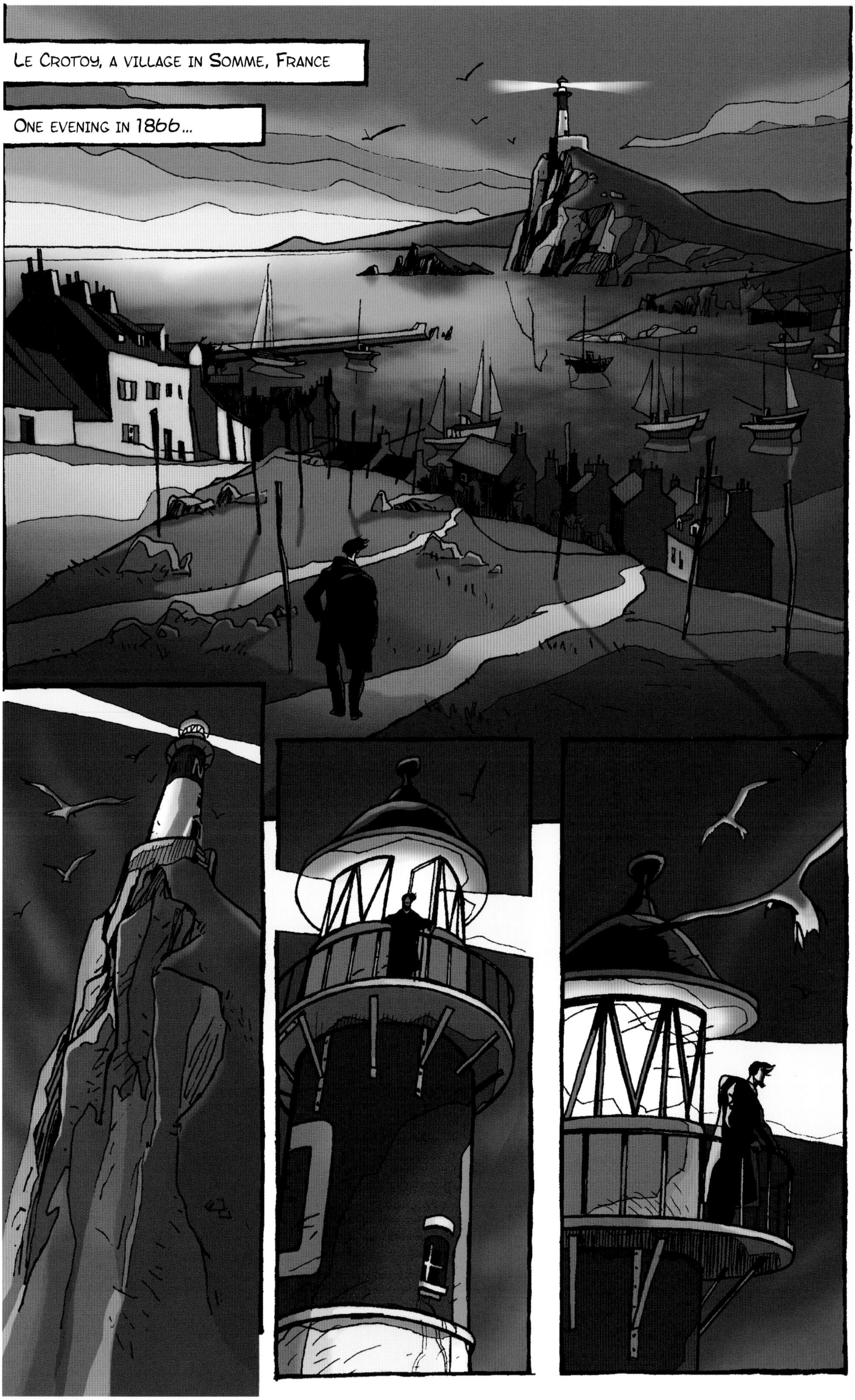
Le Crotoy, a village in Somme, France
One evening in 1866...

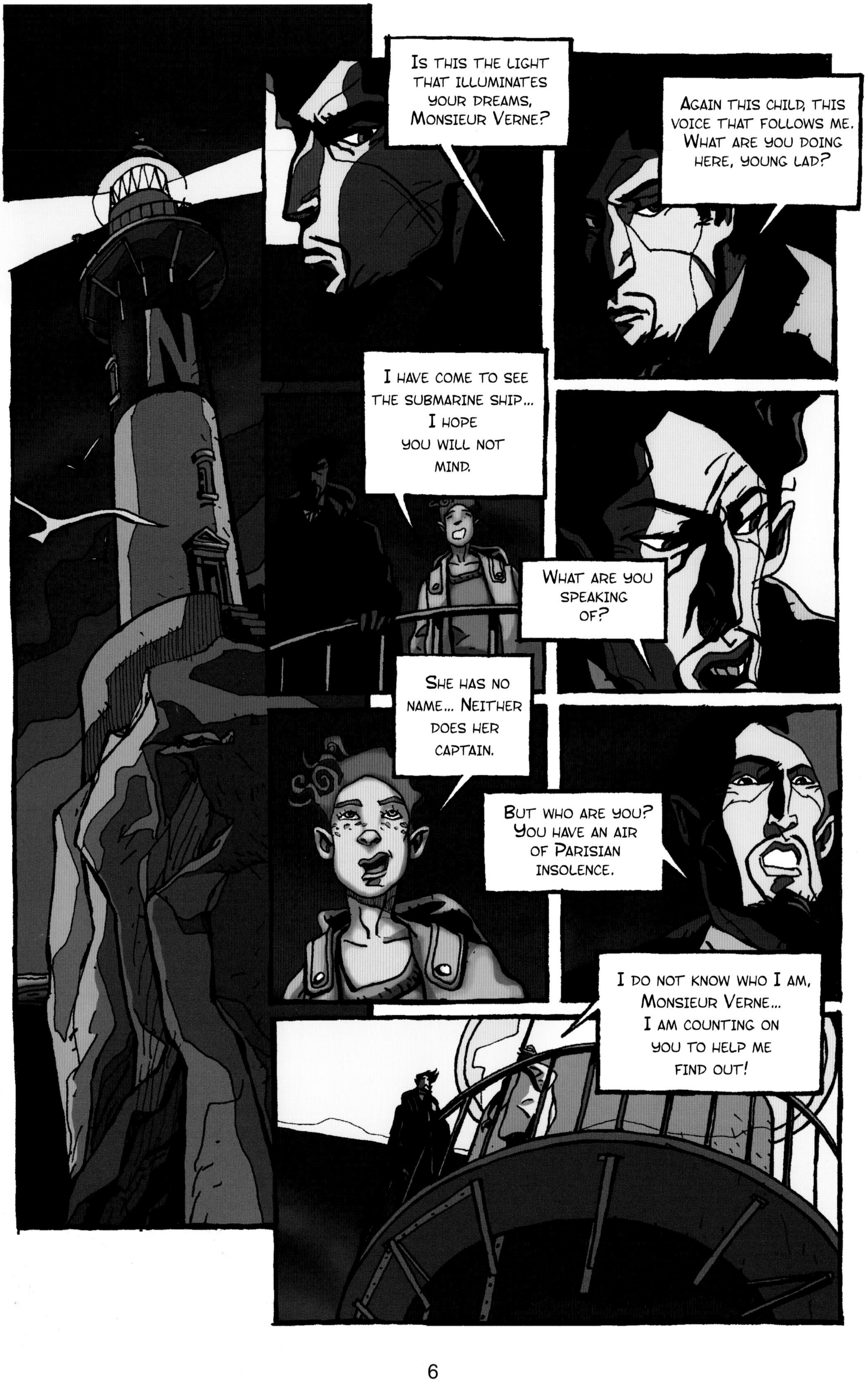

Is this the light that illuminates your dreams, Monsieur Verne?
Again this child, this voice that follows me. What are you doing here, young lad?
I have come to see the submarine ship... I hope you will not mind.
What are you speaking of?
She has no name... Neither does her captain.
But who are you? You have an air of Parisian insolence.
I do not know who I am, Monsieur Verne... I am counting on you to help me find out!

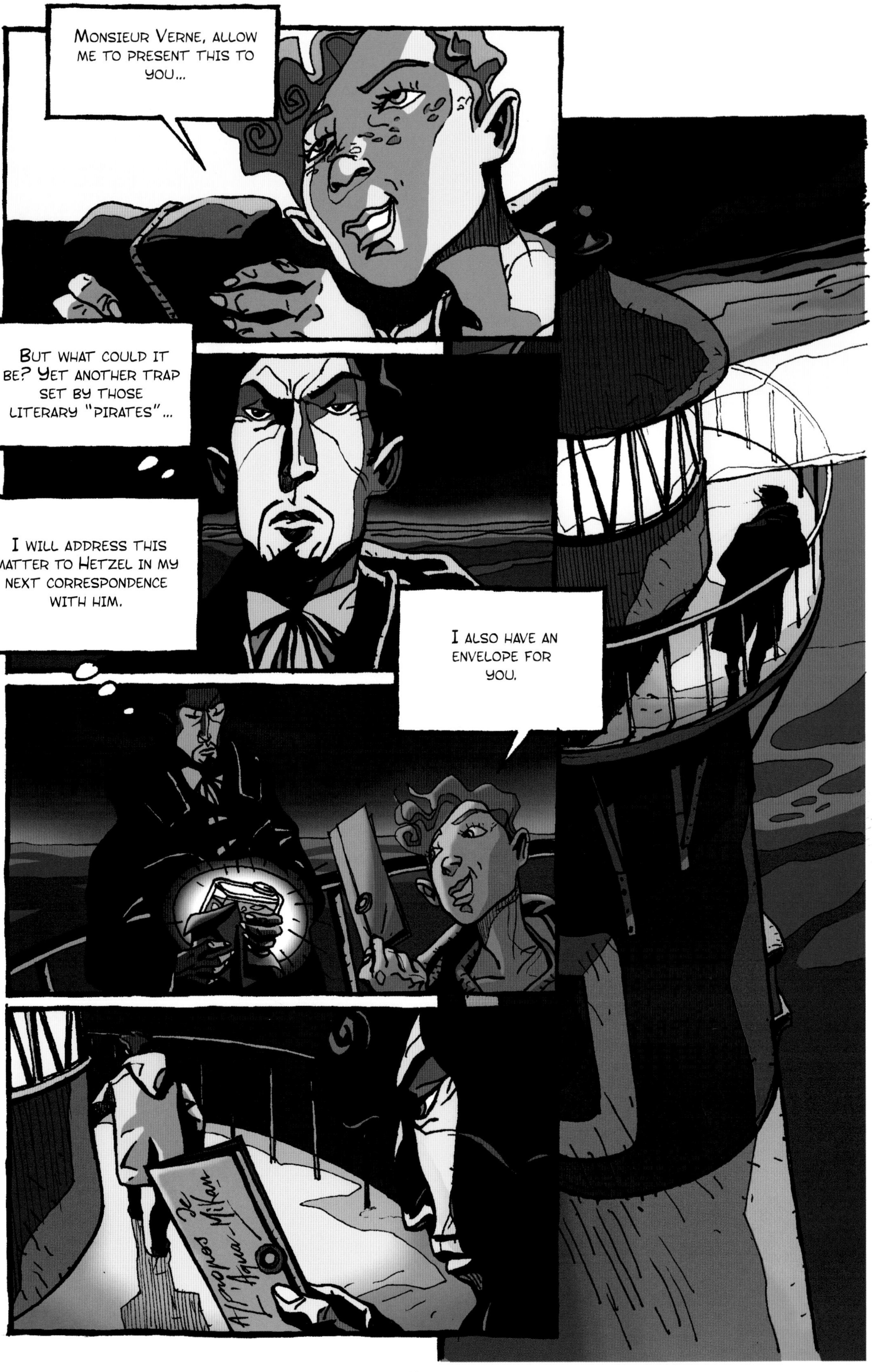
MONSIEUR VERNE, ALLOW ME TO PRESENT THIS TO YOU...
BUT WHAT COULD IT BE? YET ANOTHER TRAP SET BY THOSE LITERARY "PIRATES"...
I WILL ADDRESS THIS MATTER TO HETZEL IN MY NEXT CORRESPONDENCE WITH HIM.
I ALSO HAVE AN ENVELOPE FOR YOU.

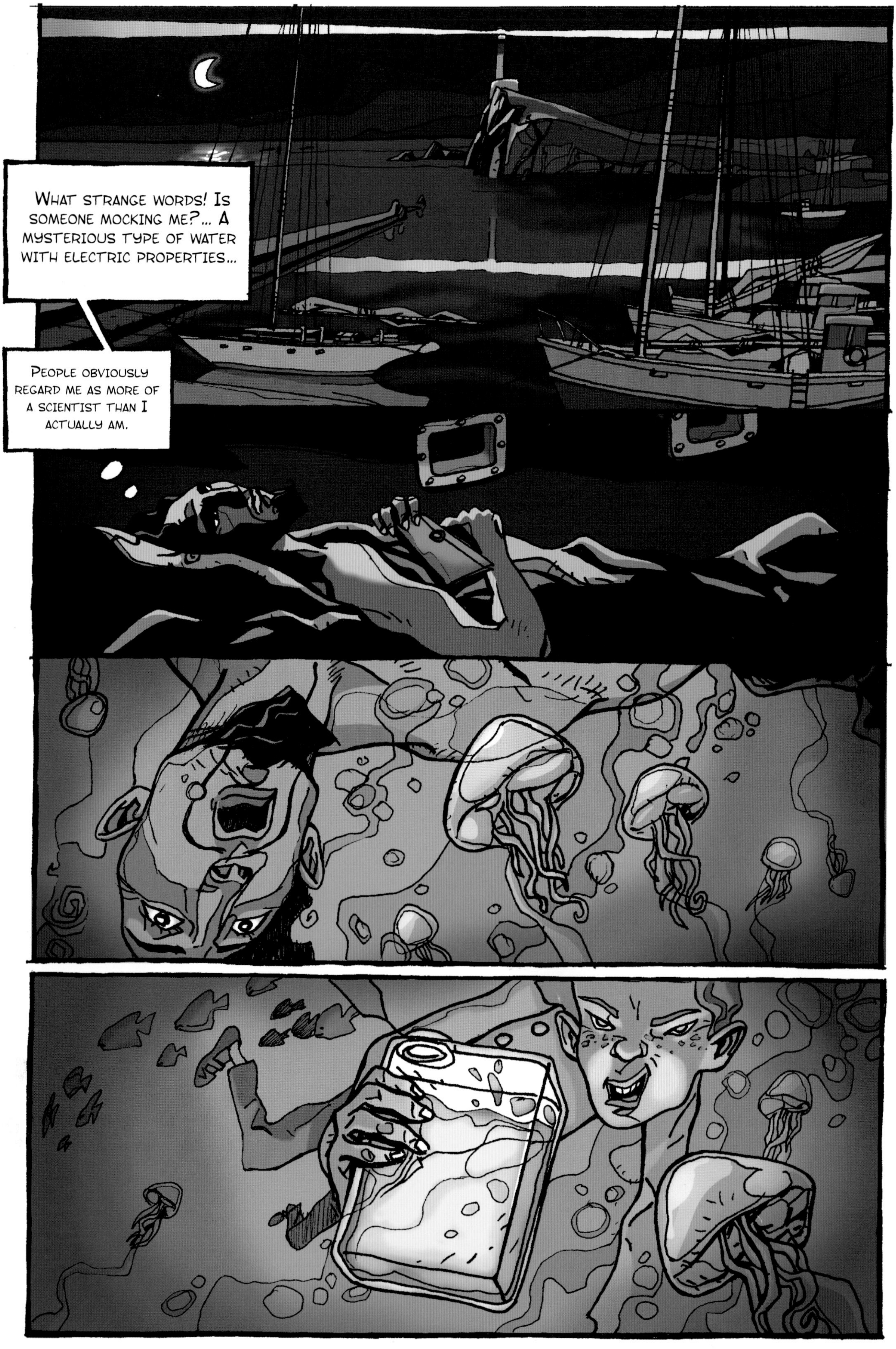
What strange words! Is someone mocking me?... A mysterious type of water with electric properties...
People obviously regard me as more of a scientist than I actually am.

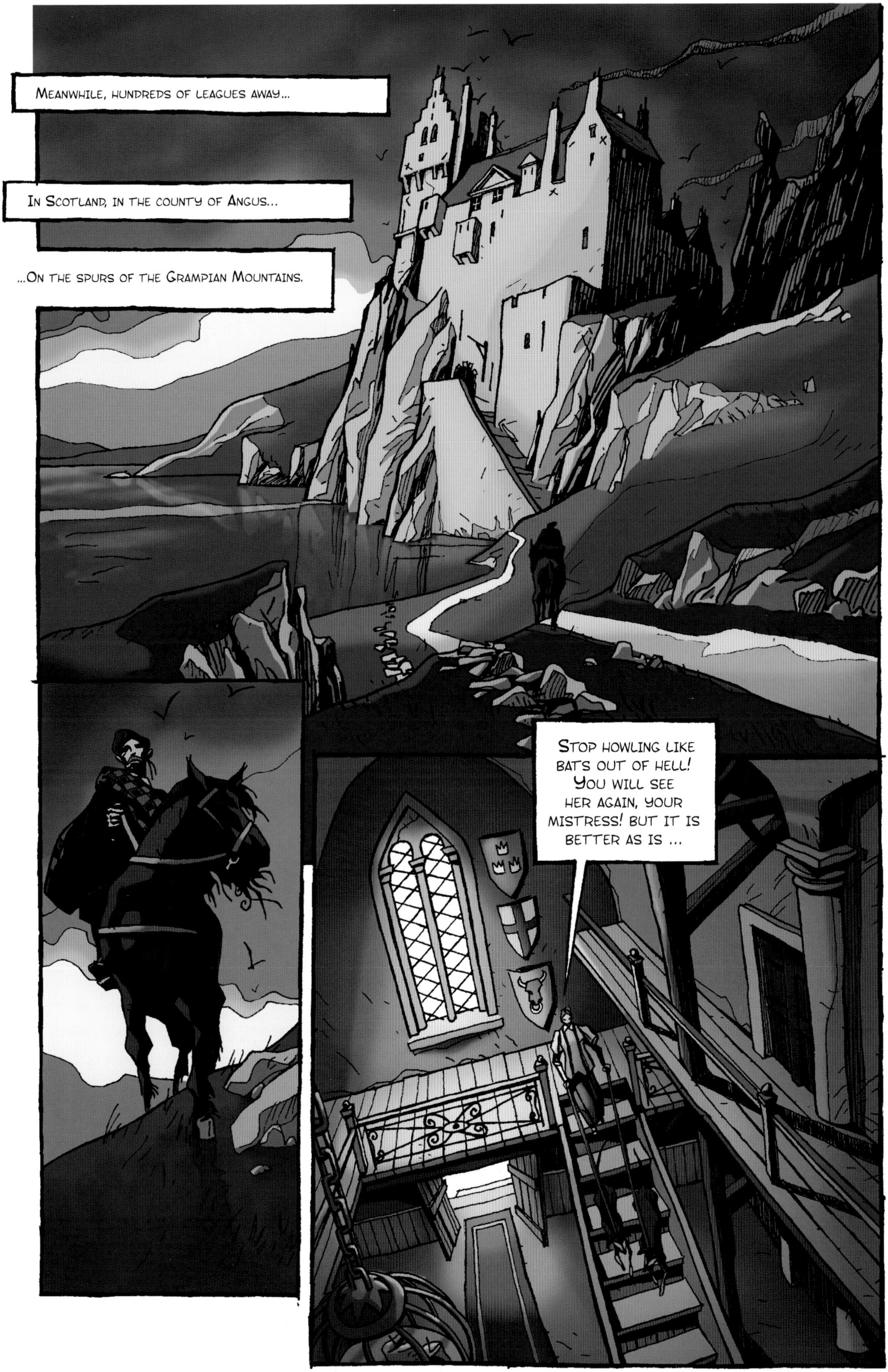
MEANWHILE, HUNDREDS OF LEAGUES AWAY...
IN SCOTLAND, IN THE COUNTY OF ANGUS...
...ON THE SPURS OF THE GRAMPIAN MOUNTAINS.
STOP HOWLING LIKE BATS OUT OF HELL! YOU WILL SEE HER AGAIN, YOUR MISTRESS! BUT IT IS BETTER AS IS ...

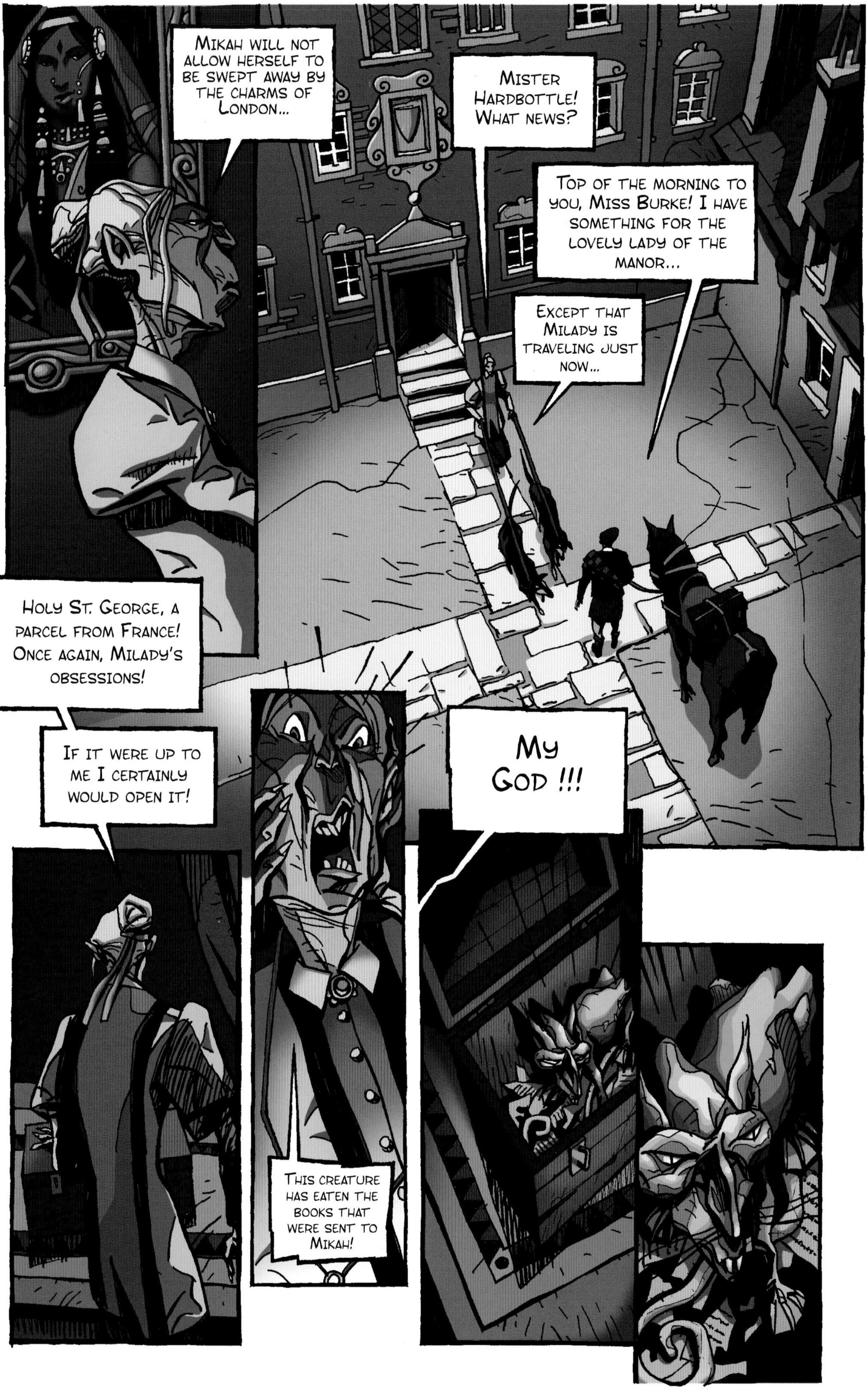
Mikah will not allow herself to be swept away by the charms of London...
Mister Hardbottle! What news?
Top of the morning to you, Miss Burke! I have something for the lovely lady of the manor...
Except that Milady is traveling just now...
Holy St. George, a parcel from France! Once again, Milady's obsessions!
If it were up to me I certainly would open it!
This creature has eaten the books that were sent to Mikah!
My God !!!

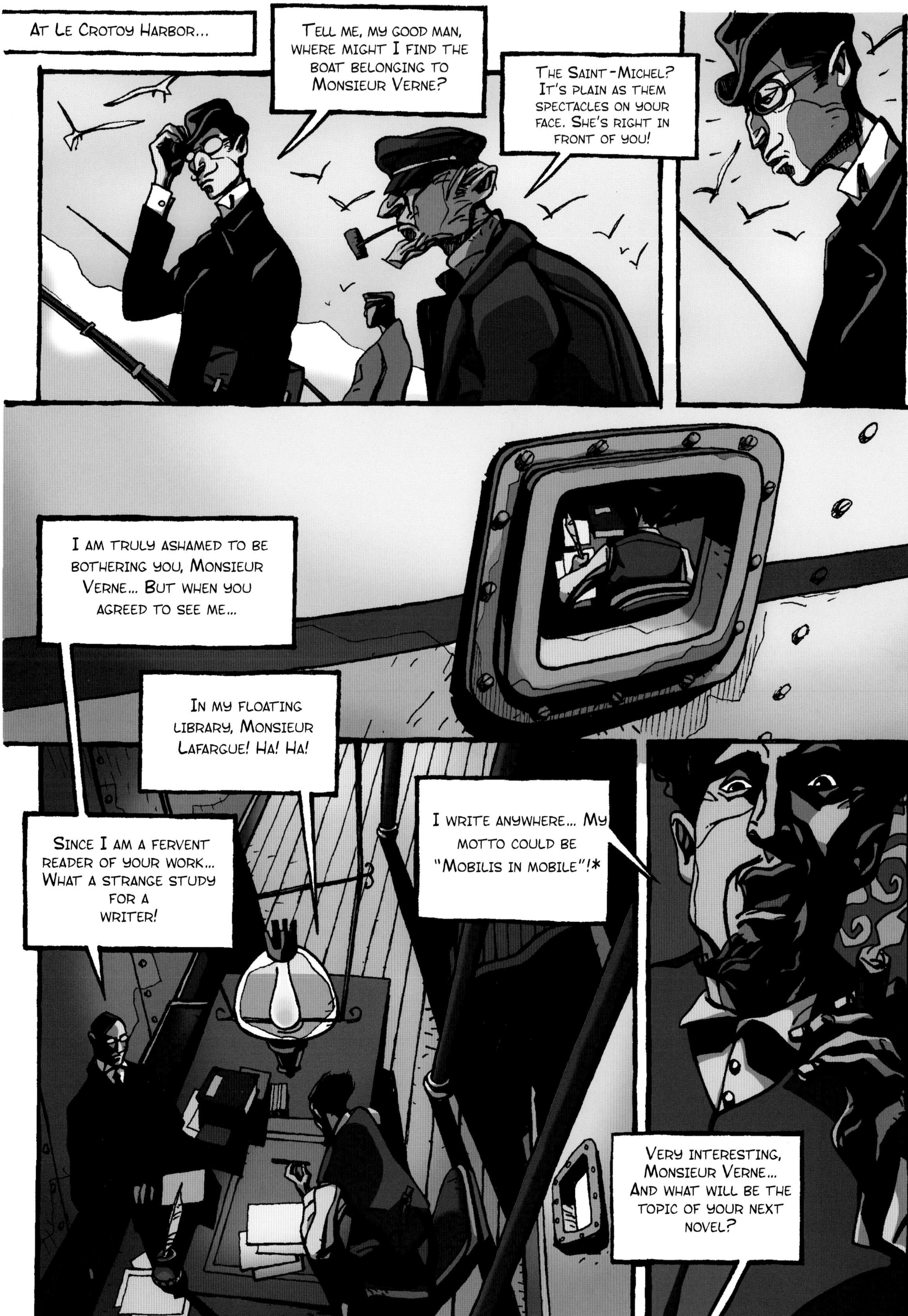
At Le Crotoy Harbor...
Tell me, my good man, where might I find the boat belonging to Monsieur Verne?
The Saint-Michel? It's plain as them spectacles on your face. She's right in front of you!
I am truly ashamed to be bothering you, Monsieur Verne... But when you agreed to see me...
In my floating library, Monsieur Lafargue! Ha! Ha!
Since I am a fervent reader of your work... What a strange study for a writer!
I write anywhere... My motto could be "Mobilis in mobile"!*
Very interesting, Monsieur Verne... And what will be the topic of your next novel?

* In motion within motion.

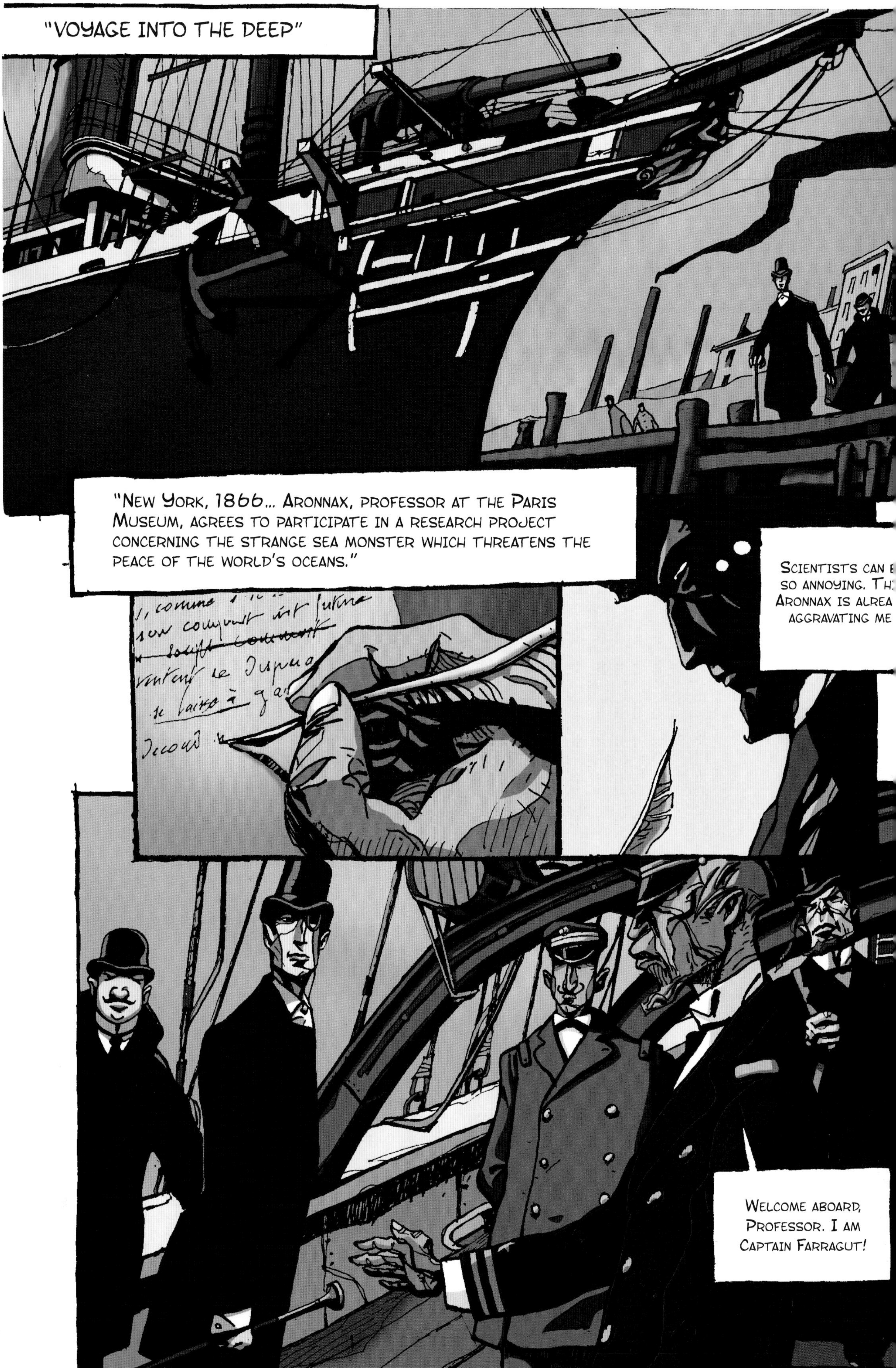
"VOYAGE INTO THE DEEP"
"NEW YORK, 1866... ARONNAX, PROFESSOR AT THE PARIS MUSEUM, AGREES TO PARTICIPATE IN A RESEARCH PROJECT CONCERNING THE STRANGE SEA MONSTER WHICH THREATENS THE PEACE OF THE WORLD'S OCEANS."
SCIENTISTS CAN B SO ANNOYING. TH ARONNAX IS ALREA AGGRAVATING ME
WELCOME ABOARD, PROFESSOR. I AM CAPTAIN FARRAGUT!

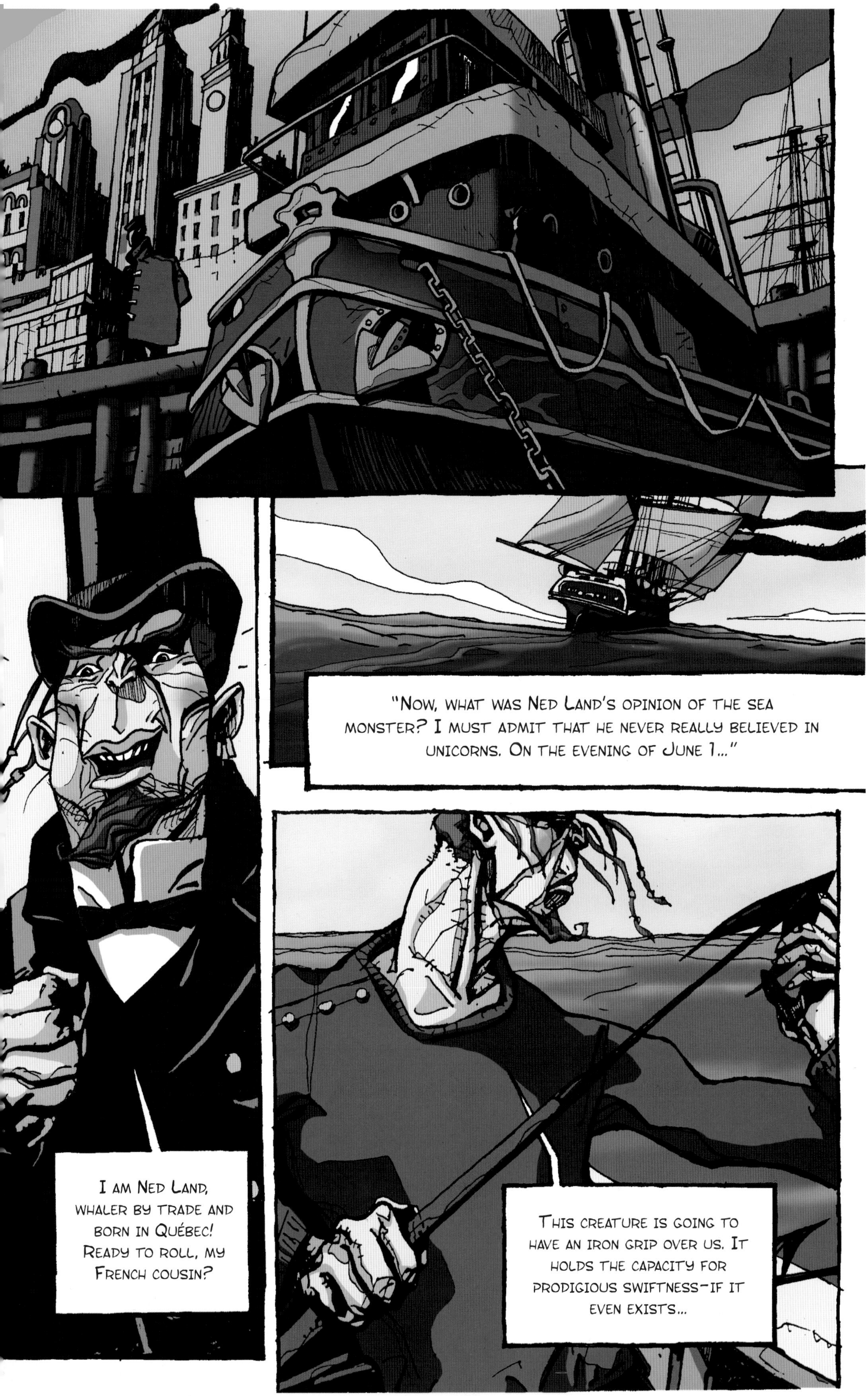
I AM NED LAND, WHALER BY TRADE AND BORN IN QUÉBEC! READY TO ROLL, MY FRENCH COUSIN?
"NOW, WHAT WAS NED LAND'S OPINION OF THE SEA MONSTER? I MUST ADMIT THAT HE NEVER REALLY BELIEVED IN UNICORNS. ON THE EVENING OF JUNE 1..."
THIS CREATURE IS GOING TO HAVE AN IRON GRIP OVER US. IT HOLDS THE CAPACITY FOR PRODIGIOUS SWIFTNESS—IF IT EVEN EXISTS...

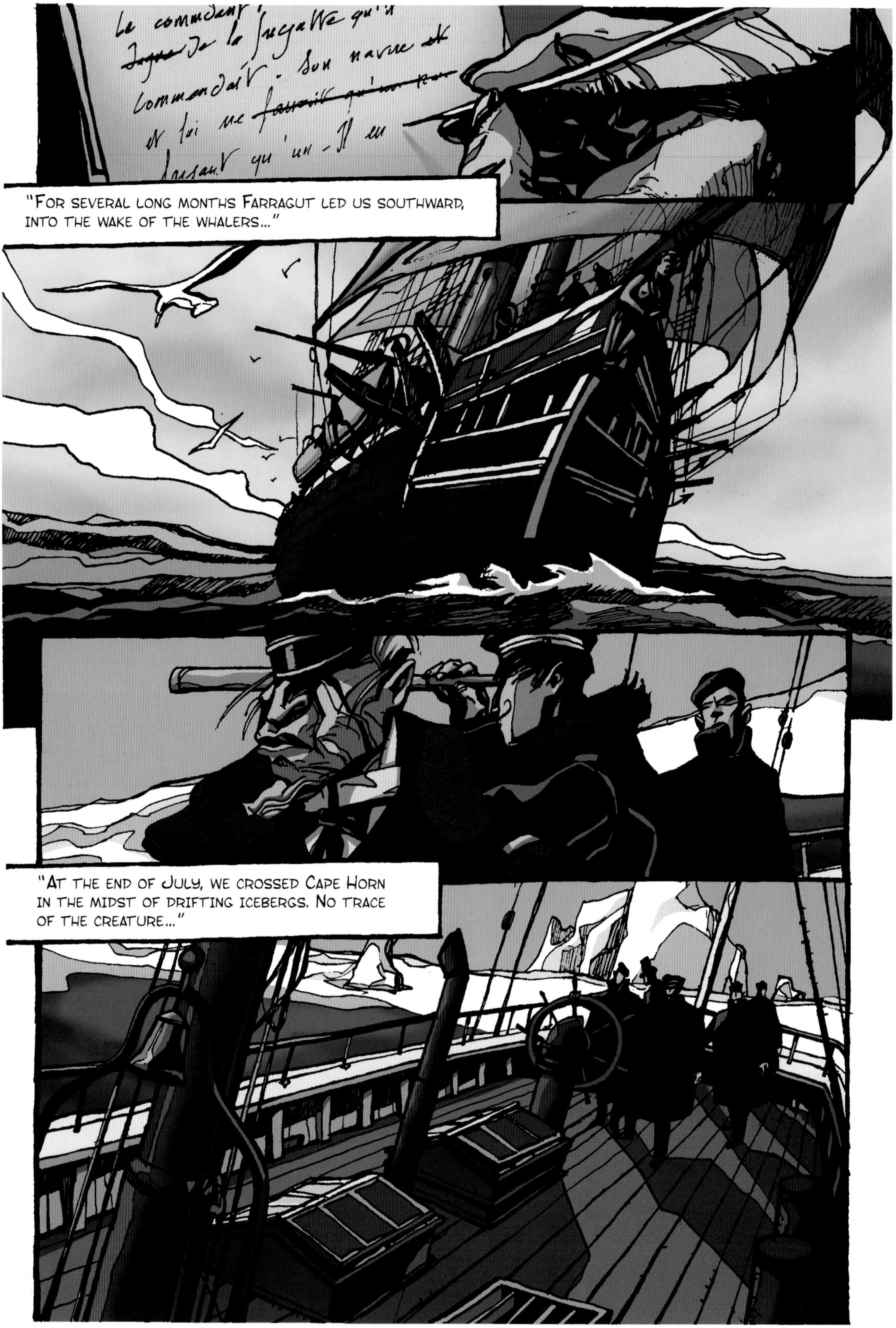
"For several long months Farragut led us southward, into the wake of the whalers..."
"At the end of July, we crossed Cape Horn in the midst of drifting icebergs. No trace of the creature..."

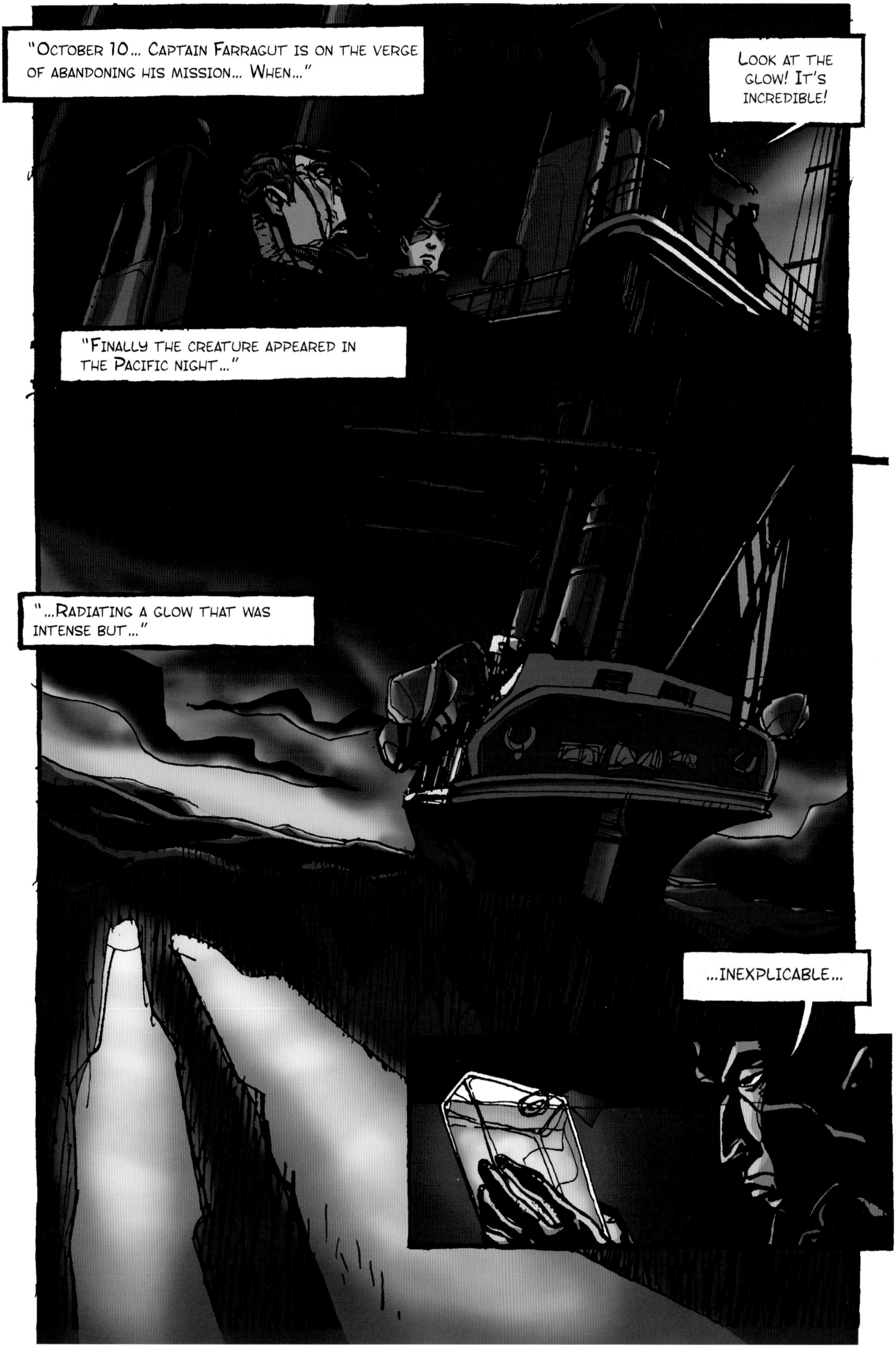
"October 10... Captain Farragut is on the verge of abandoning his mission... When..."
Look at the glow! It's incredible!
"Finally the creature appeared in the Pacific night..."
"...Radiating a glow that was intense but..."
...inexplicable...

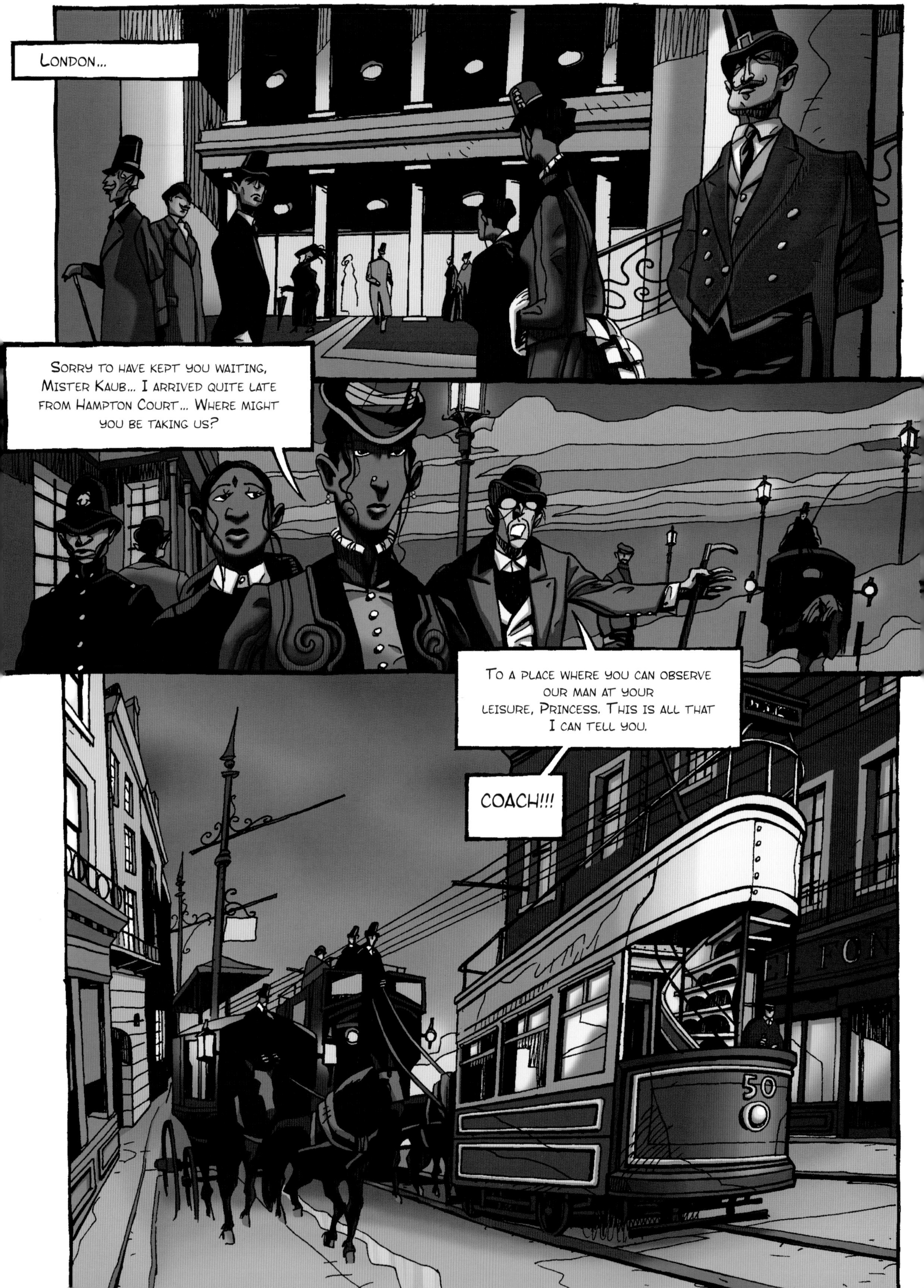
LONDON...
SORRY TO HAVE KEPT YOU WAITING, MISTER KAUB... I ARRIVED QUITE LATE FROM HAMPTON COURT... WHERE MIGHT YOU BE TAKING US?
TO A PLACE WHERE YOU CAN OBSERVE OUR MAN AT YOUR LEISURE, PRINCESS. THIS IS ALL THAT I CAN TELL YOU.
COACH!!!
50

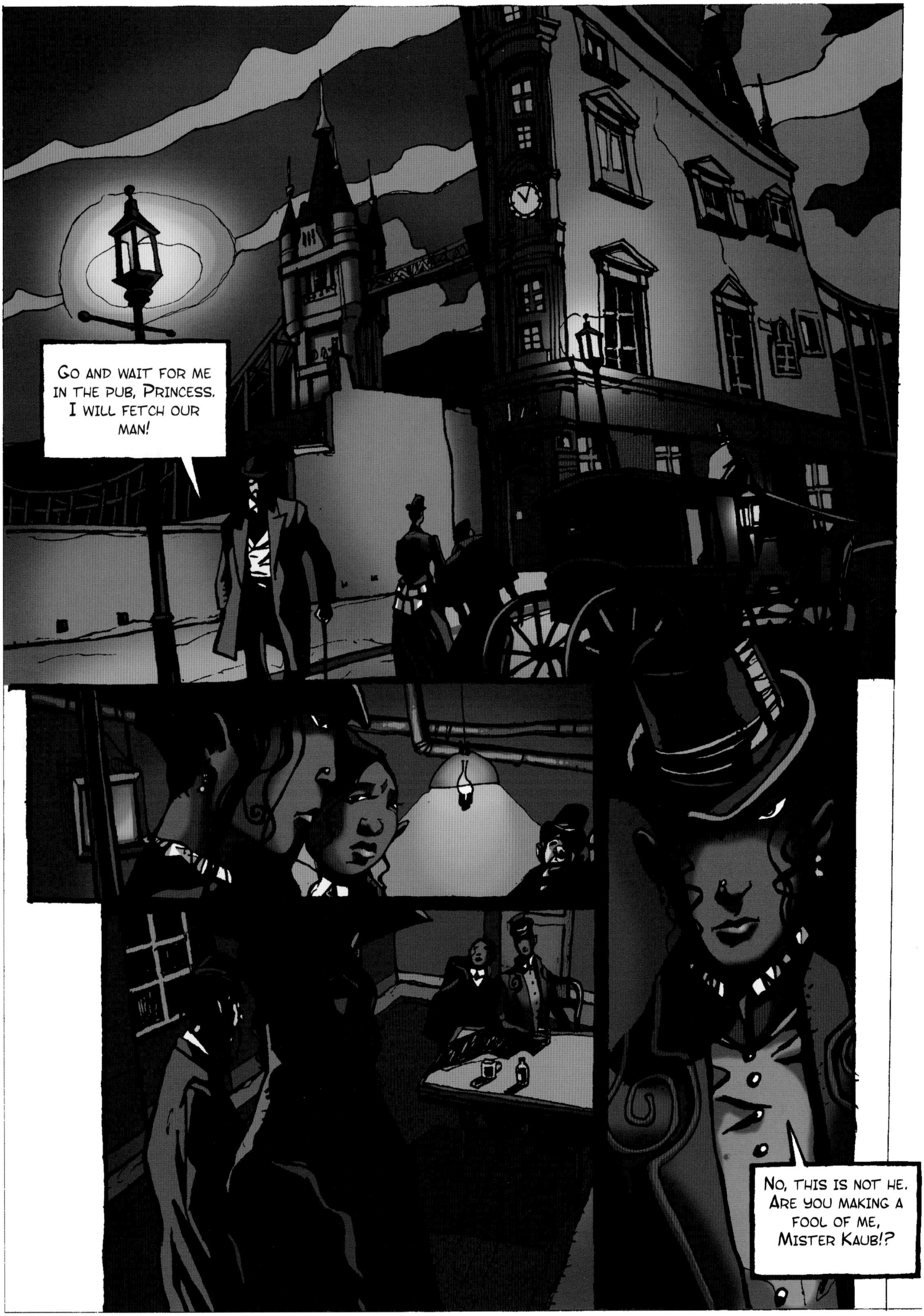
GO AND WAIT FOR ME IN THE PUB, PRINCESS. I WILL FETCH OUR MAN!
NO, THIS IS NOT HE. ARE YOU MAKING A FOOL OF ME, MISTER KAUB!?

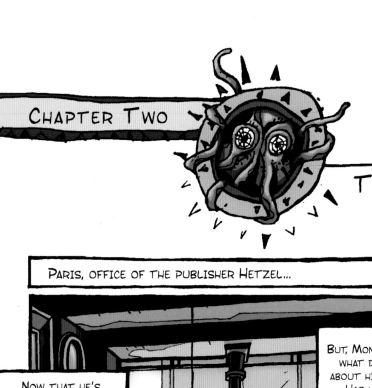

Chapter Two

The Sarcophagus Club

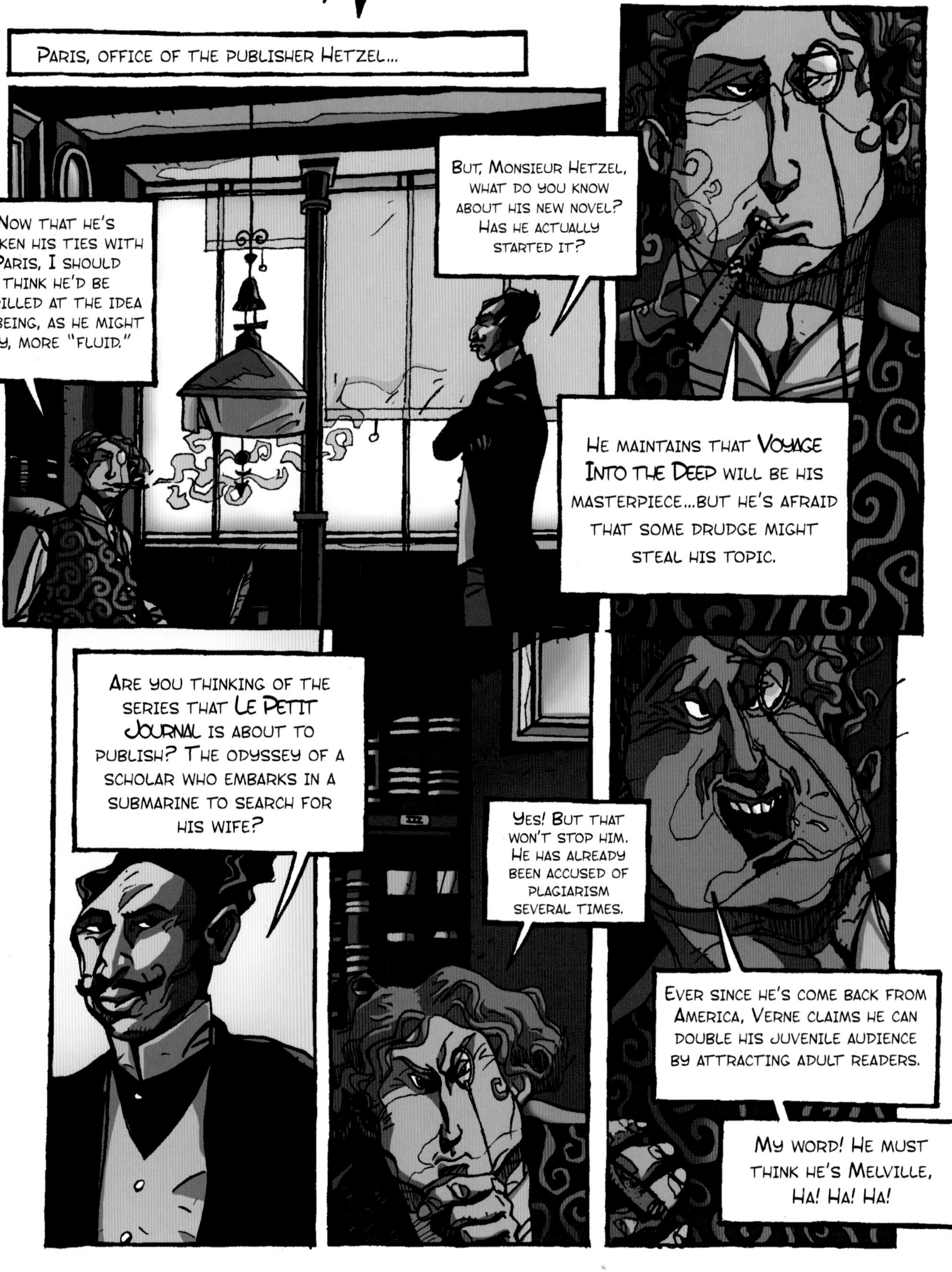

Paris, office of the publisher Hetzel...
Now that he's broken his ties with Paris, I should think he'd be thrilled at the idea of being, as he might say, more "fluid."
But, Monsieur Hetzel, what do you know about his new novel? Has he actually started it?
He maintains that Voyage Into the Deep will be his masterpiece...but he's afraid that some drudge might steal his topic.
Are you thinking of the series that Le Petit Journal is about to publish? The odyssey of a scholar who embarks in a submarine to search for his wife?
Yes! But that won't stop him. He has already been accused of plagiarism several times.
Ever since he's come back from America, Verne claims he can double his juvenile audience by attracting adult readers.
My word! He must think he's Melville, Ha! Ha! Ha!

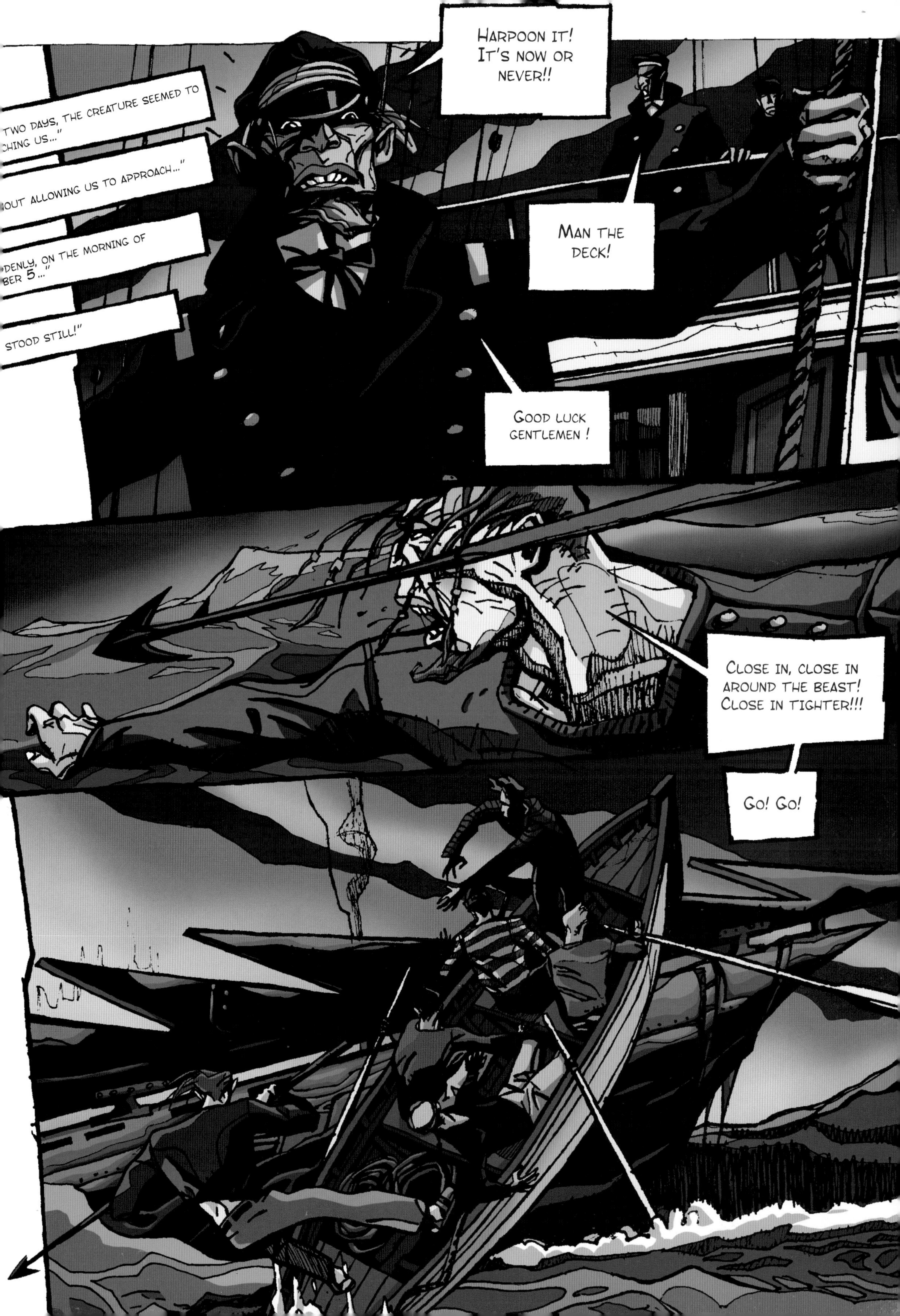

TWO DAYS, THE CREATURE SEEMED TO
CHING US..."
IOUT ALLOWING US TO APPROACH..."
DENLY, ON THE MORNING OF
BER 5..."
STOOD STILL!"
HARPOON IT! IT'S NOW OR NEVER!!
MAN THE DECK!
GOOD LUCK GENTLEMEN !
CLOSE IN, CLOSE IN AROUND THE BEAST! CLOSE IN TIGHTER!!!
GO! GO!

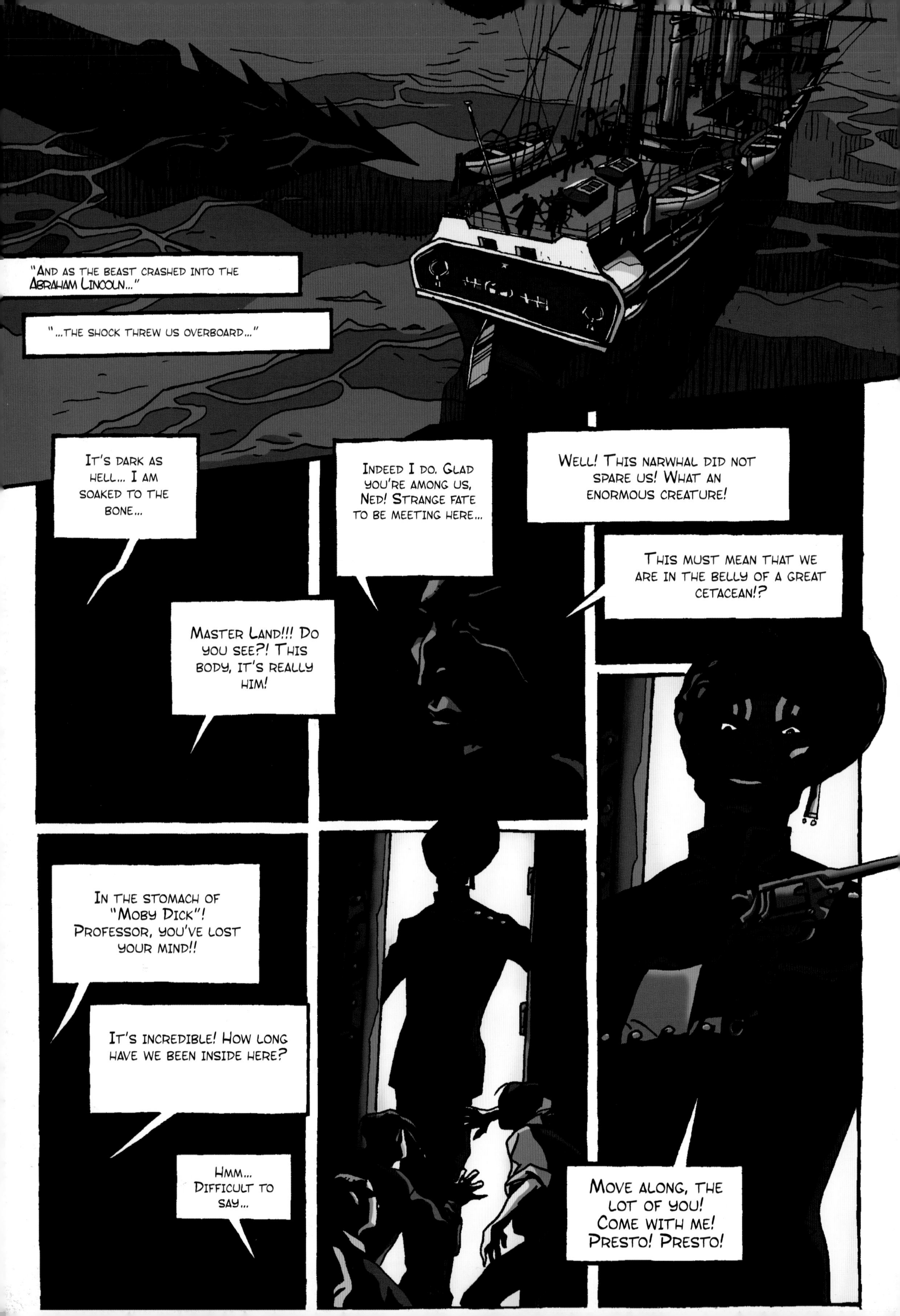
"And as the beast crashed into the Abraham Lincoln..."
"...the shock threw us overboard..."
It's dark as hell... I am soaked to the bone...
Master Land!!! Do you see?! This body, it's really him!
Indeed I do. Glad you're among us, Ned! Strange fate to be meeting here...
Well! This narwhal did not spare us! What an enormous creature!
This must mean that we are in the belly of a great cetacean!?
In the stomach of "Moby Dick"! Professor, you've lost your mind!!
It's incredible! How long have we been inside here?
Hmm... Difficult to say...
Move along, the lot of you! Come with me! Presto! Presto!

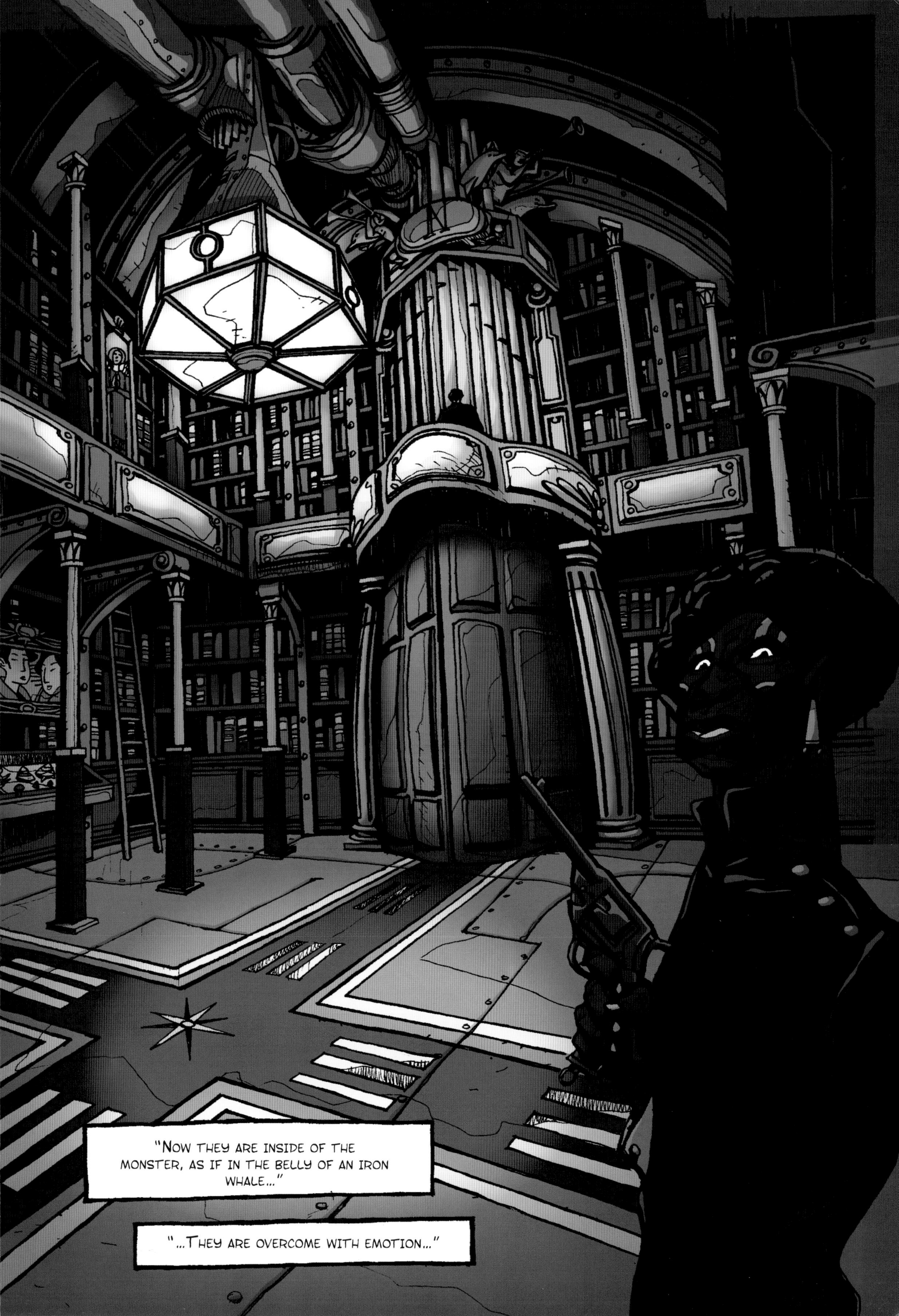
"Now they are inside of the monster, as if in the belly of an iron whale..."
"...They are overcome with emotion..."

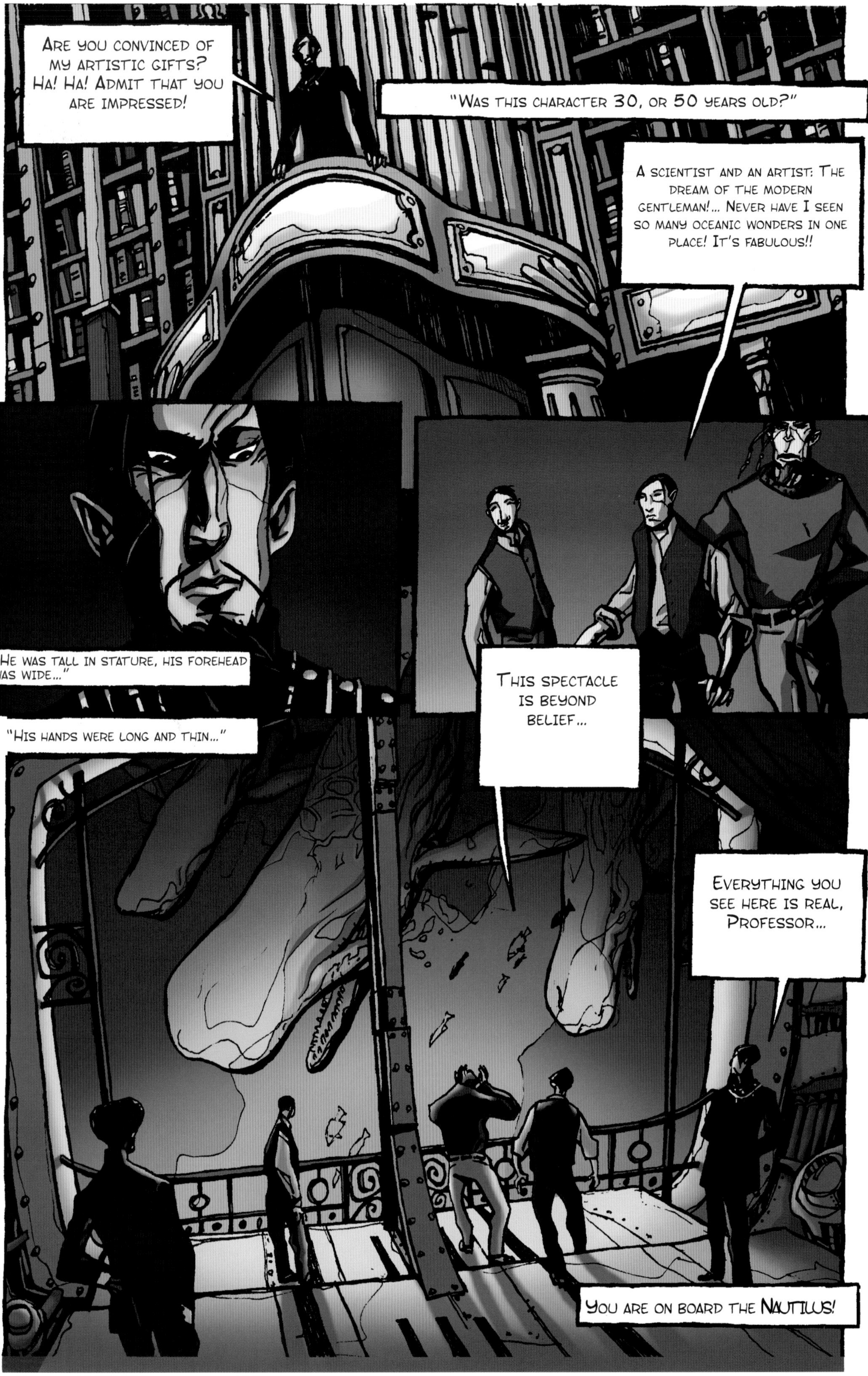
Are you convinced of my artistic gifts? Ha! Ha! Admit that you are impressed!
"Was this character 30, or 50 years old?"
A scientist and an artist: The dream of the modern gentleman!... Never have I seen so many oceanic wonders in one place! It's fabulous!!
"He was tall in stature, his forehead was wide..."
This spectacle is beyond belief...
"His hands were long and thin..."
Everything you see here is real, Professor...
You are on board the Nautilus!

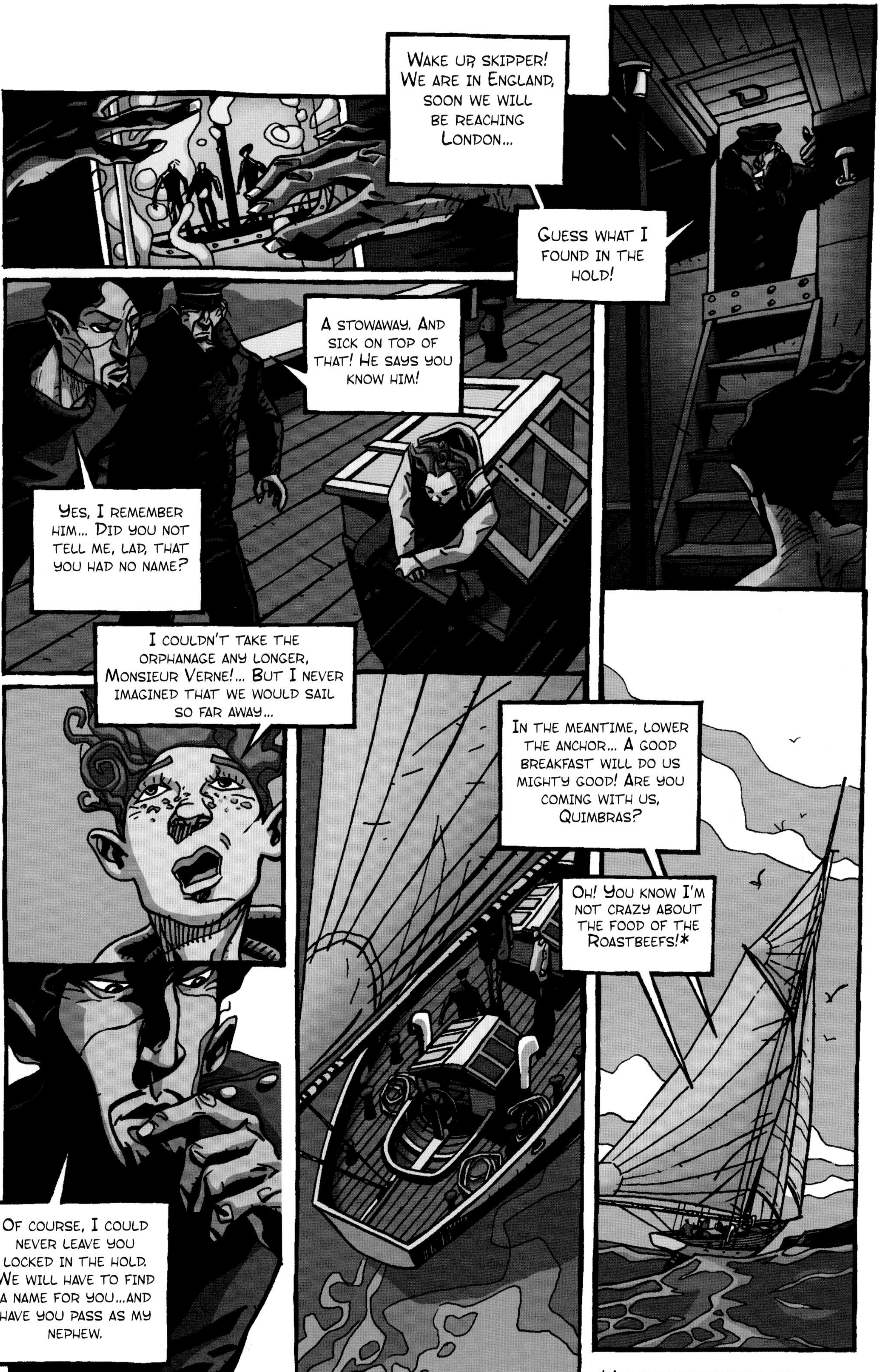
WAKE UP, SKIPPER! WE ARE IN ENGLAND, SOON WE WILL BE REACHING LONDON...
GUESS WHAT I FOUND IN THE HOLD!
A STOWAWAY. AND SICK ON TOP OF THAT! HE SAYS YOU KNOW HIM!
YES, I REMEMBER HIM... DID YOU NOT TELL ME, LAD, THAT YOU HAD NO NAME?
I COULDN'T TAKE THE ORPHANAGE ANY LONGER, MONSIEUR VERNE!... BUT I NEVER IMAGINED THAT WE WOULD SAIL SO FAR AWAY...
OF COURSE, I COULD NEVER LEAVE YOU LOCKED IN THE HOLD. WE WILL HAVE TO FIND A NAME FOR YOU...AND HAVE YOU PASS AS MY NEPHEW.
IN THE MEANTIME, LOWER THE ANCHOR... A GOOD BREAKFAST WILL DO US MIGHTY GOOD! ARE YOU COMING WITH US, QUIMBRAS?
OH! YOU KNOW I'M NOT CRAZY ABOUT THE FOOD OF THE ROASTBEEFS!*

*A DEROGATORY NAME FOR THE ENGLISH

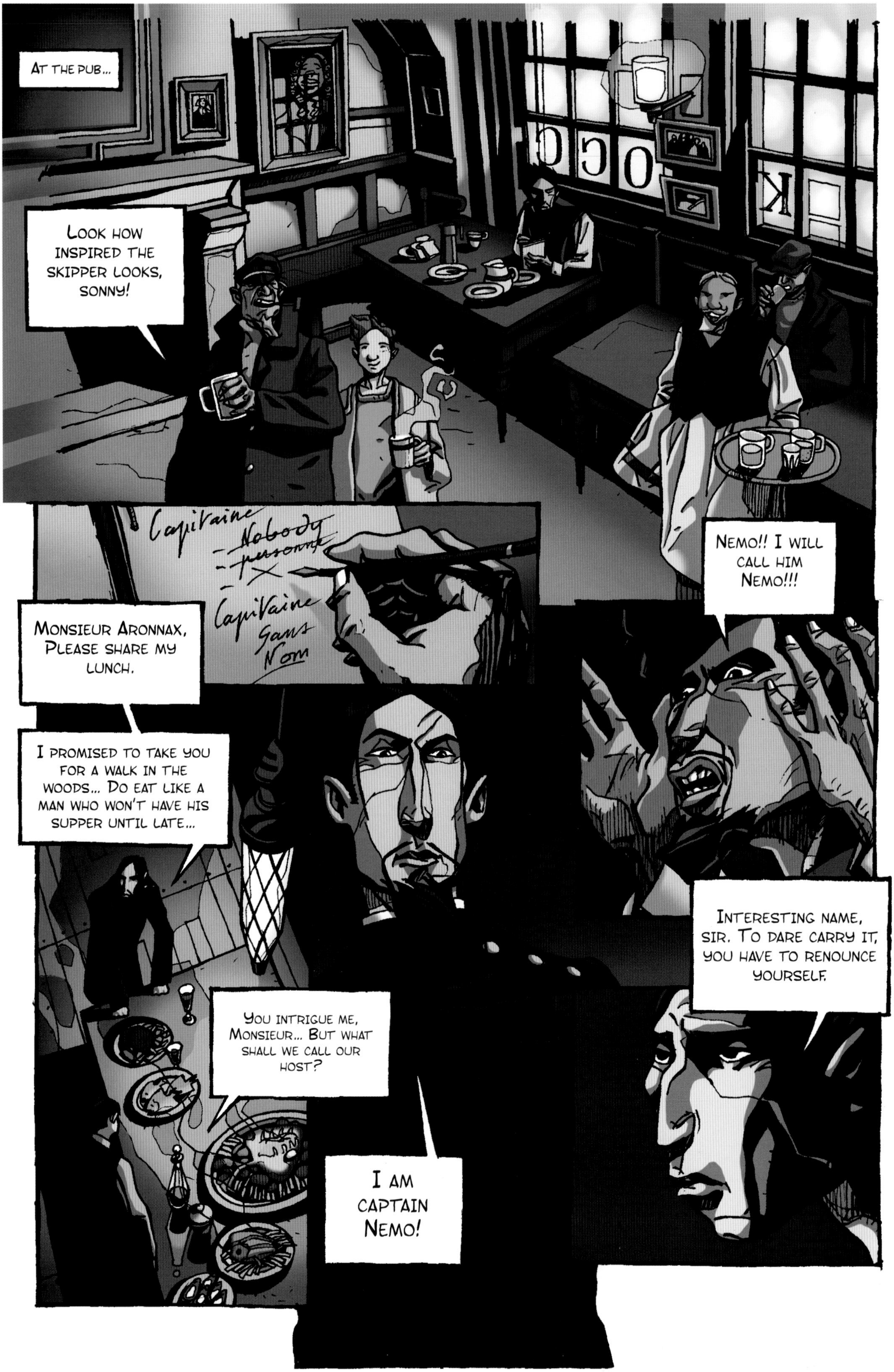
At the pub...
Look how inspired the skipper looks, sonny!
Capitaine
Nobody
personne
X
Capitaine Sans Nom
Nemo!! I will call him Nemo!!!
Monsieur Aronnax, please share my lunch.
I promised to take you for a walk in the woods... Do eat like a man who won't have his supper until late...
You intrigue me, Monsieur... But what shall we call our host?
I am Captain Nemo!
Interesting name, sir. To dare carry it, you have to renounce yourself.

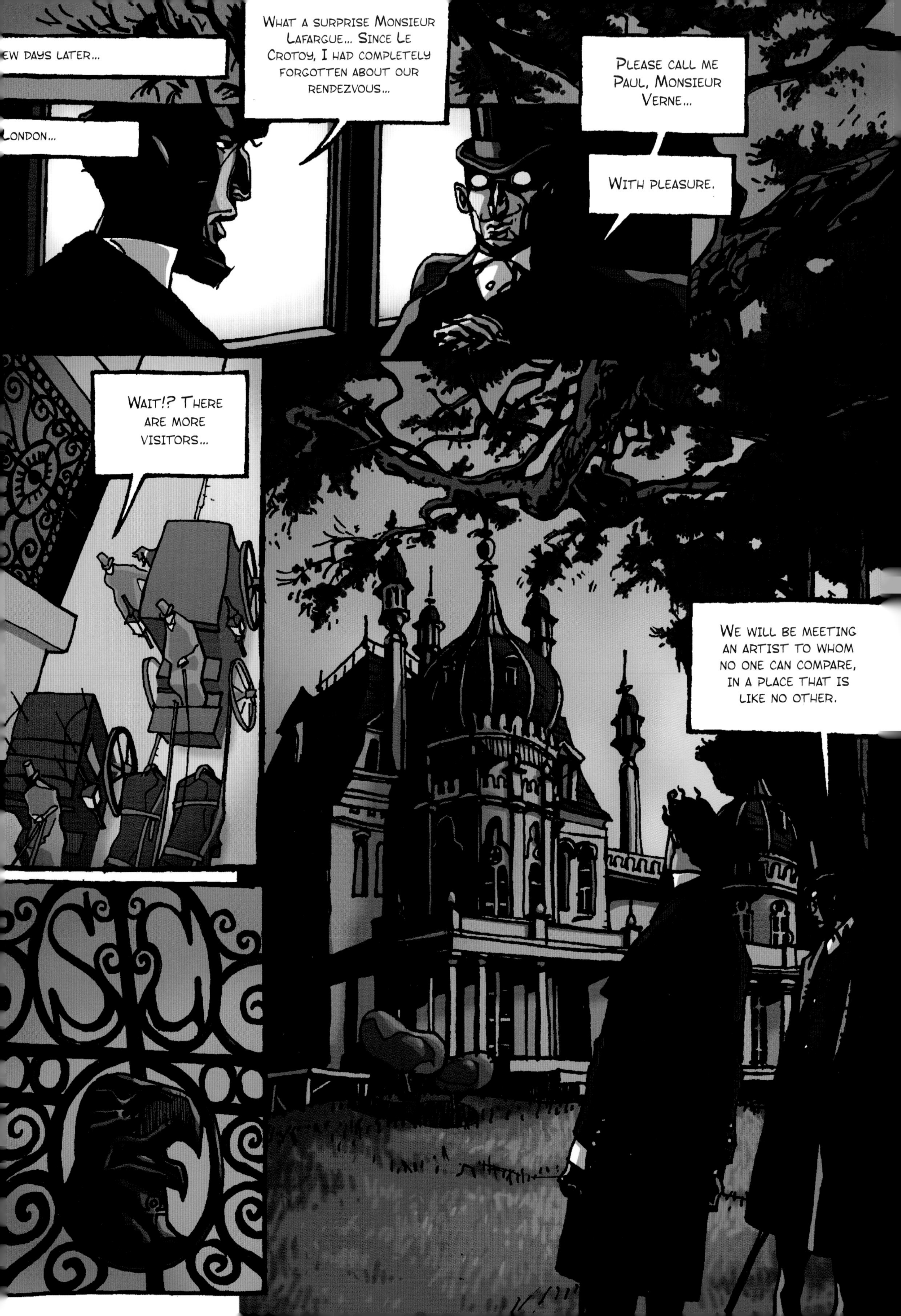
EW DAYS LATER...
LONDON...
WHAT A SURPRISE MONSIEUR LAFARGUE... SINCE LE CROTOY, I HAD COMPLETELY FORGOTTEN ABOUT OUR RENDEZVOUS...
PLEASE CALL ME PAUL, MONSIEUR VERNE...
WITH PLEASURE.
WAIT!? THERE ARE MORE VISITORS...
WE WILL BE MEETING AN ARTIST TO WHOM NO ONE CAN COMPARE, IN A PLACE THAT IS LIKE NO OTHER.

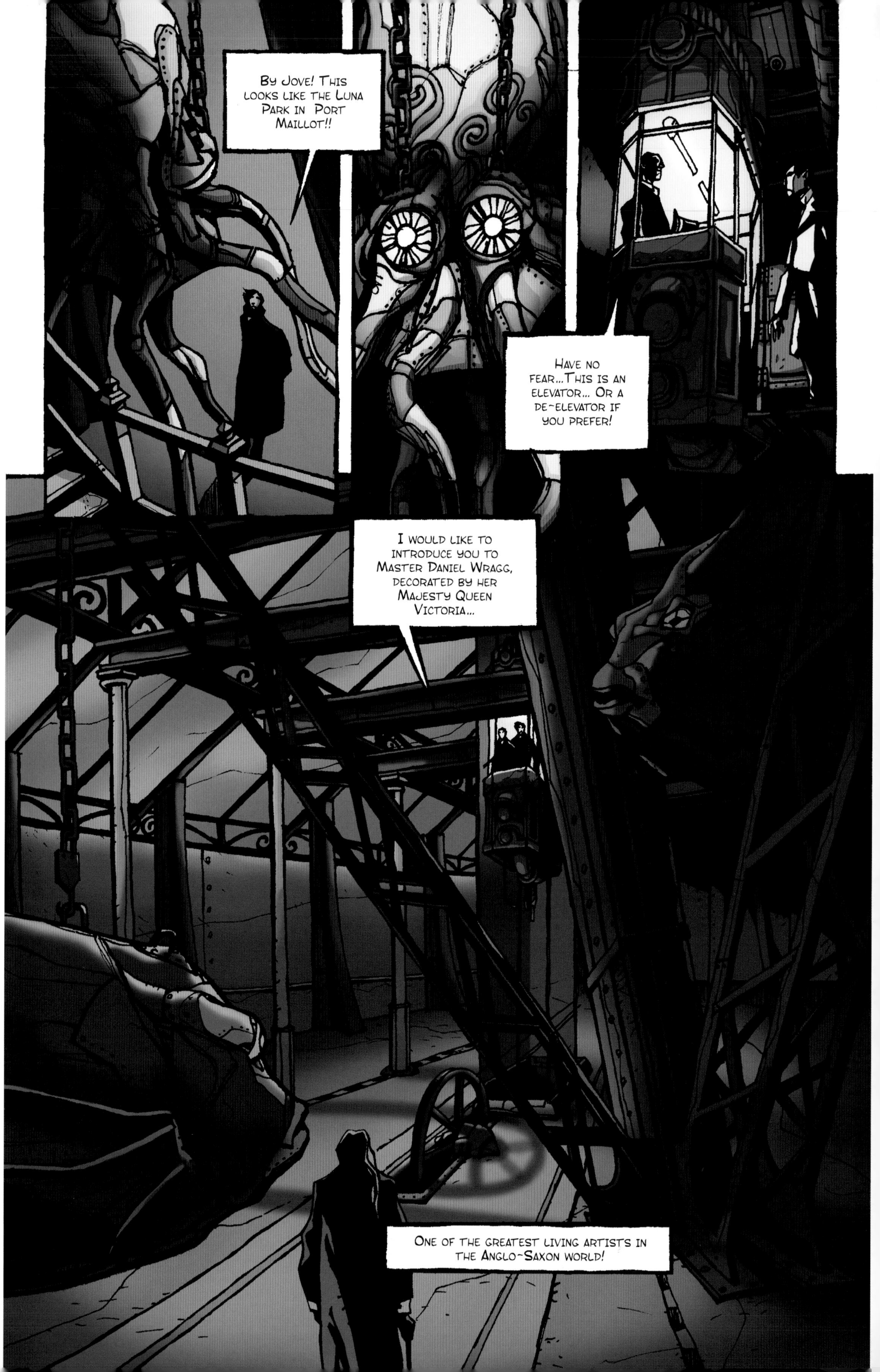
By Jove! This looks like the Luna Park in Port Maillot!!
Have no fear...This is an elevator... Or a de-elevator if you prefer!
I would like to introduce you to Master Daniel Wragg, decorated by her Majesty Queen Victoria...
One of the greatest living artists in the Anglo-Saxon world!

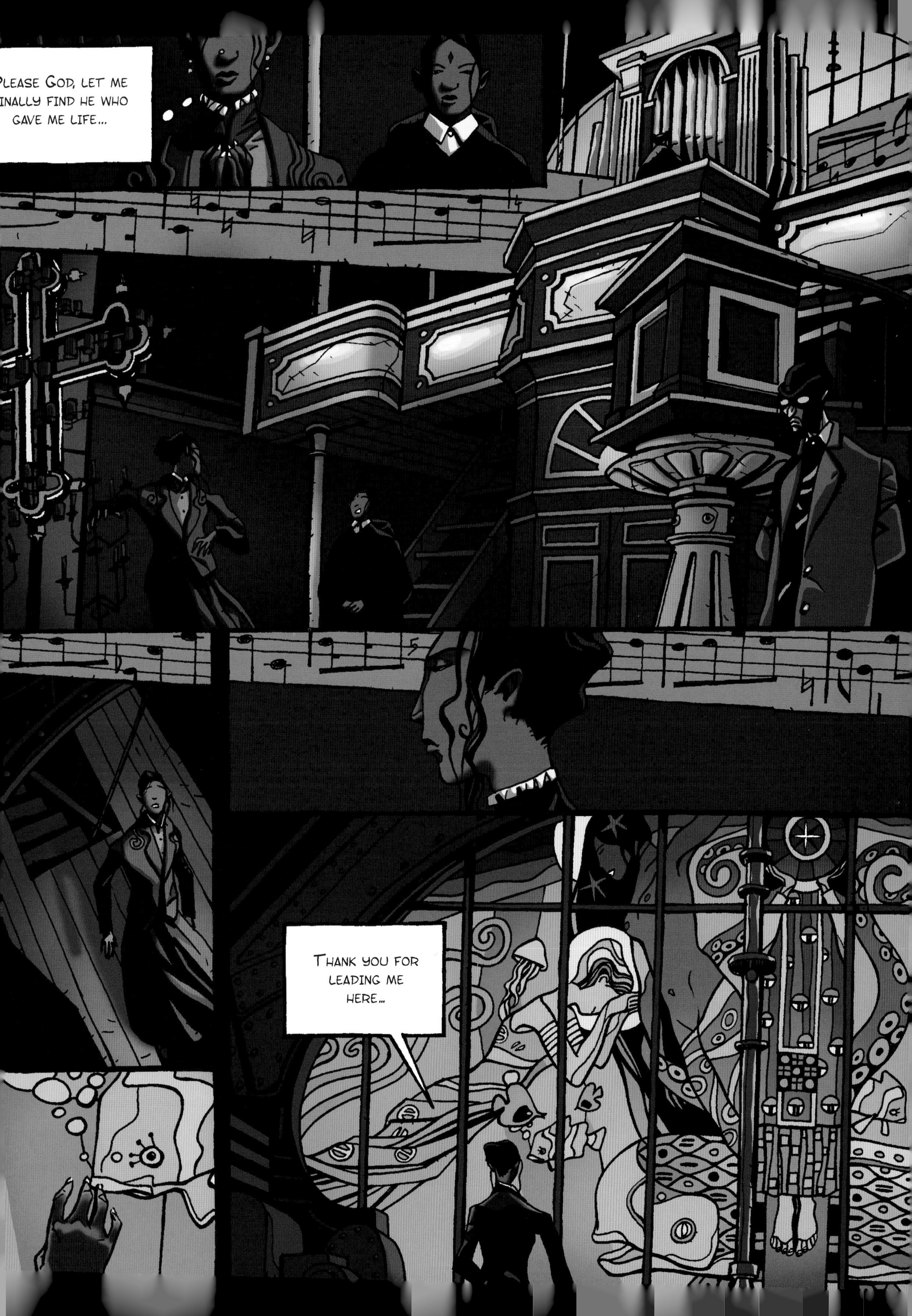

PLEASE GOD, LET ME FINALLY FIND HE WHO GAVE ME LIFE...
THANK YOU FOR LEADING ME HERE...

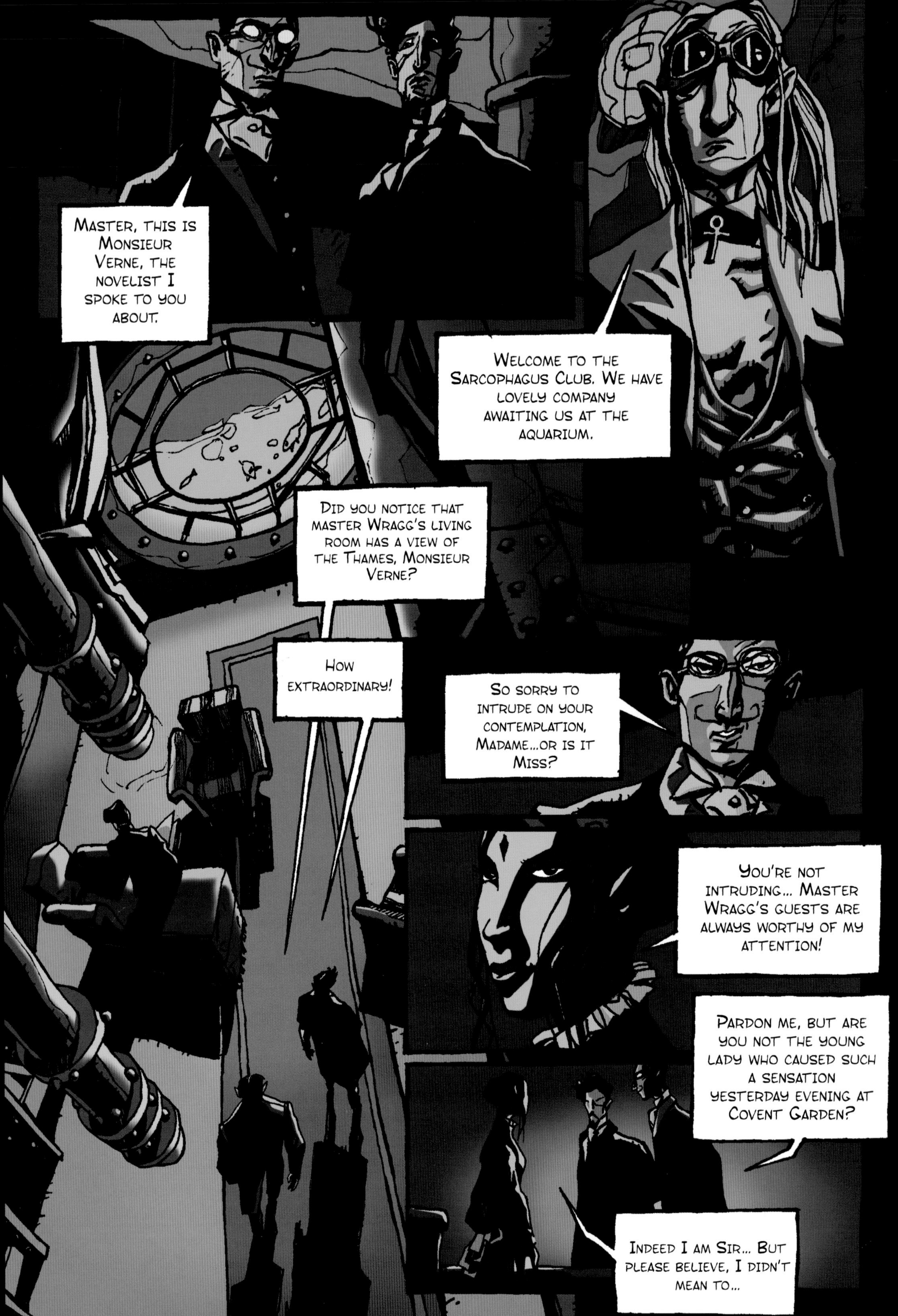
Master, this is Monsieur Verne, the novelist I spoke to you about.
Welcome to the Sarcophagus Club. We have lovely company awaiting us at the aquarium.
Did you notice that master Wragg's living room has a view of the Thames, Monsieur Verne?
How extraordinary!
So sorry to intrude on your contemplation, Madame...or is it Miss?
You're not intruding... Master Wragg's guests are always worthy of my attention!
Pardon me, but are you not the young lady who caused such a sensation yesterday evening at Covent Garden?
Indeed I am Sir... But please believe, I didn't mean to...

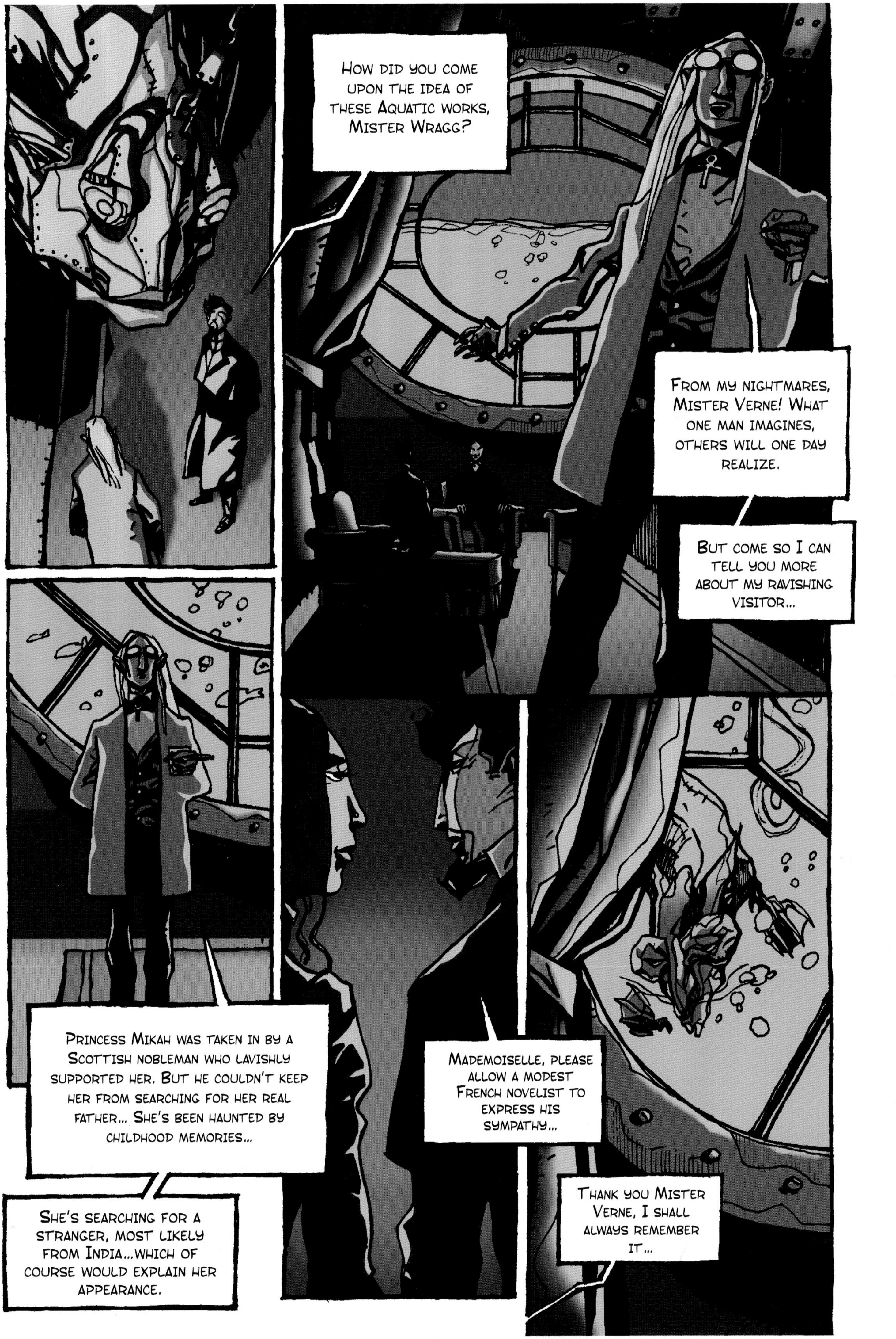
How did you come upon the idea of these Aquatic works, Mister Wragg?
From my nightmares, Mister Verne! What one man imagines, others will one day realize.
But come so I can tell you more about my ravishing visitor...
Princess Mikah was taken in by a Scottish nobleman who lavishly supported her. But he couldn't keep her from searching for her real father... She's been haunted by childhood memories...
She's searching for a stranger, most likely from India...which of course would explain her appearance.
Mademoiselle, please allow a modest French novelist to express his sympathy...
Thank you Mister Verne, I shall always remember it...

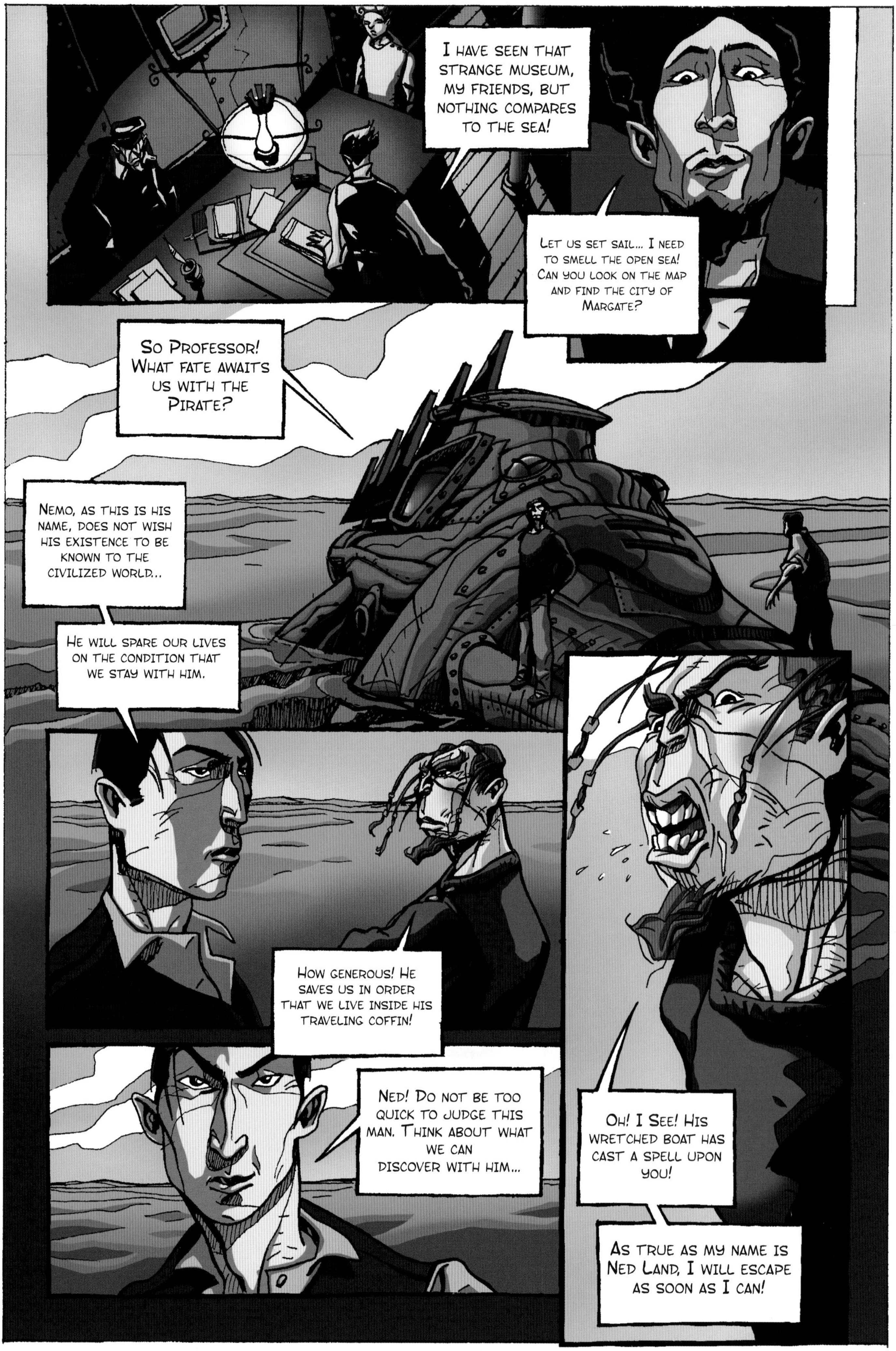

I HAVE SEEN THAT STRANGE MUSEUM, MY FRIENDS, BUT NOTHING COMPARES TO THE SEA!
LET US SET SAIL... I NEED TO SMELL THE OPEN SEA! CAN YOU LOOK ON THE MAP AND FIND THE CITY OF MARGATE?
SO PROFESSOR! WHAT FATE AWAITS US WITH THE PIRATE?
NEMO, AS THIS IS HIS NAME, DOES NOT WISH HIS EXISTENCE TO BE KNOWN TO THE CIVILIZED WORLD...
HE WILL SPARE OUR LIVES ON THE CONDITION THAT WE STAY WITH HIM.
HOW GENEROUS! HE SAVES US IN ORDER THAT WE LIVE INSIDE HIS TRAVELING COFFIN!
NED! DO NOT BE TOO QUICK TO JUDGE THIS MAN. THINK ABOUT WHAT WE CAN DISCOVER WITH HIM...
OH! I SEE! HIS WRETCHED BOAT HAS CAST A SPELL UPON YOU!
AS TRUE AS MY NAME IS NED LAND, I WILL ESCAPE AS SOON AS I CAN!

The Meeting at Margate

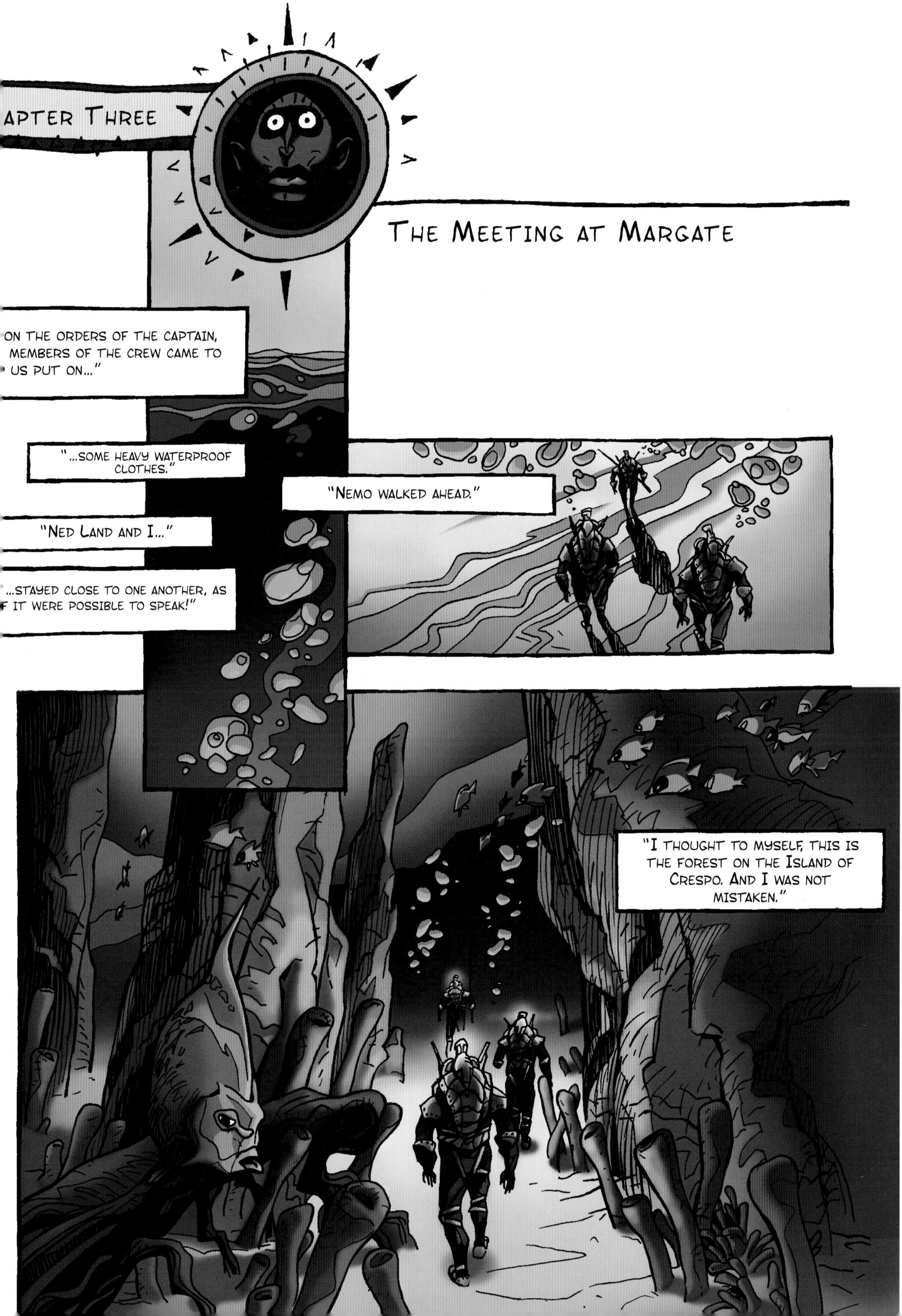

apter Three
The Meeting at Margate
"On the orders of the captain, members of the crew came to us put on..."
"...some heavy waterproof clothes."
"Nemo walked ahead."
"Ned Land and I..."
"...stayed close to one another, as f it were possible to speak!"
"I thought to myself, this is the forest on the Island of Crespo. And I was not mistaken."

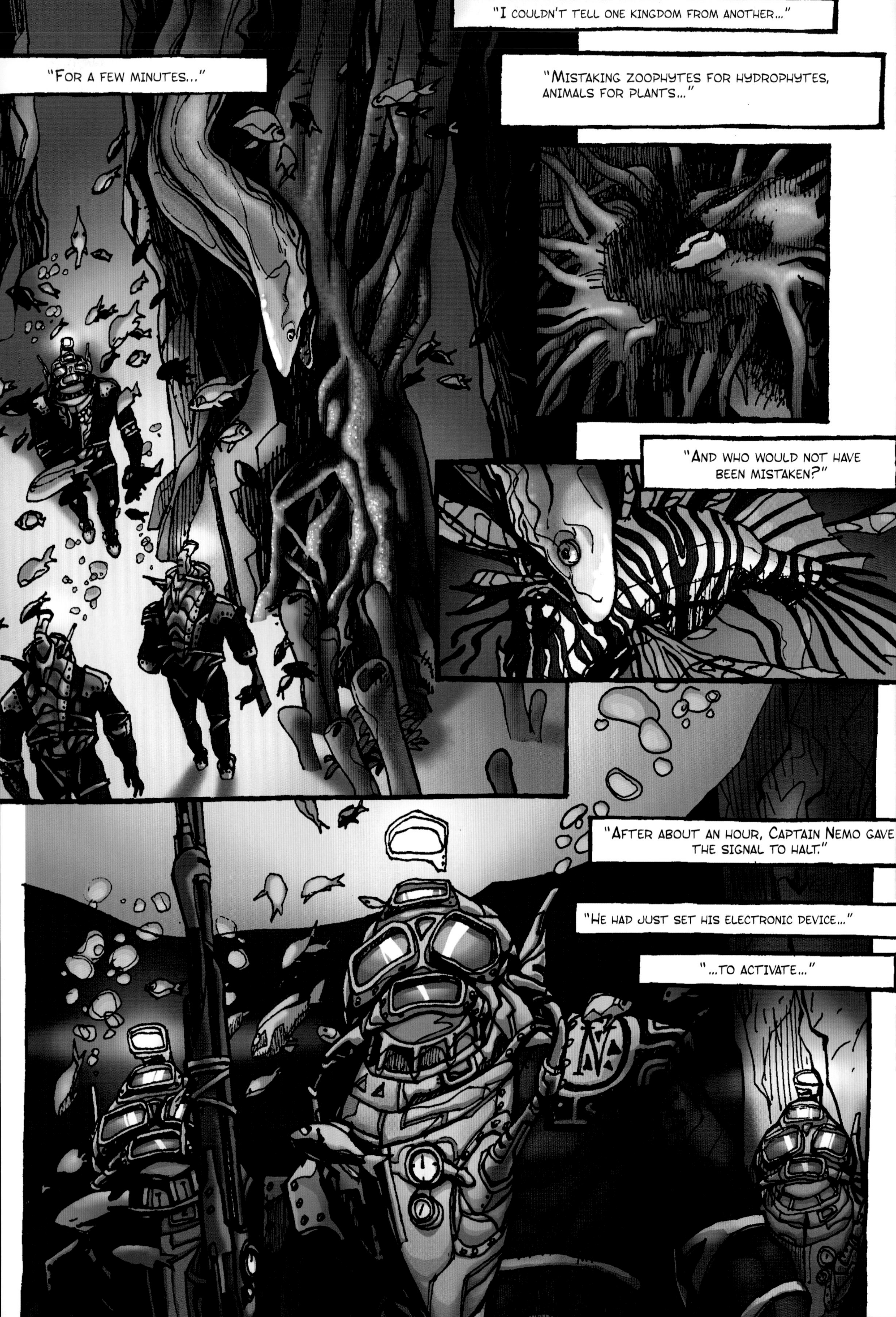
"I couldn't tell one kingdom from another..."
"For a few minutes..."
"Mistaking zoophytes for hydrophytes, animals for plants..."
"And who would not have been mistaken?"
"After about an hour, Captain Nemo gave the signal to halt."
"He had just set his electronic device..."
"...to activate..."

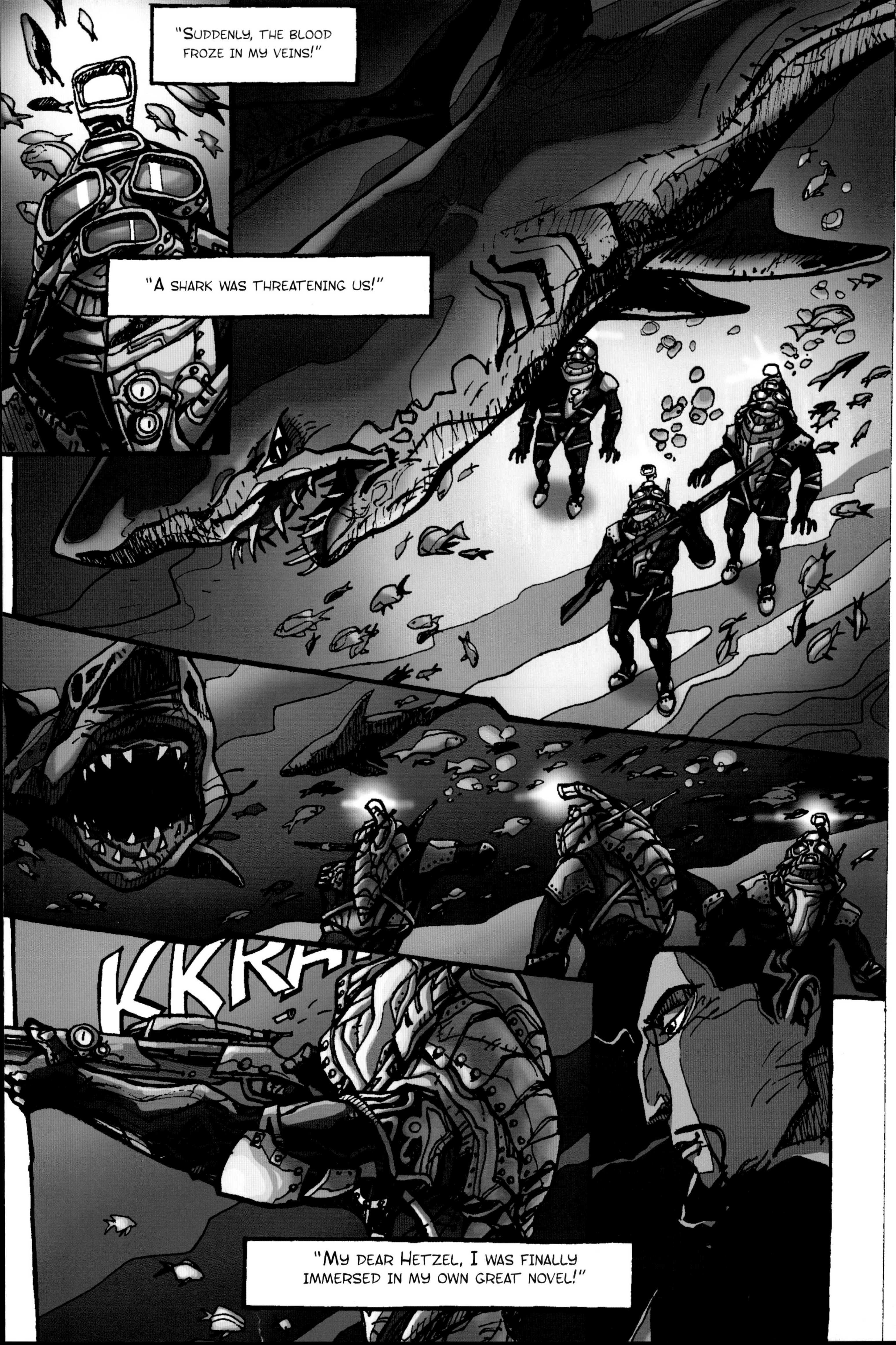
"Suddenly, the blood froze in my veins!"
"A shark was threatening us!"
KKRA
"My dear Hetzel, I was finally immersed in my own great novel!"

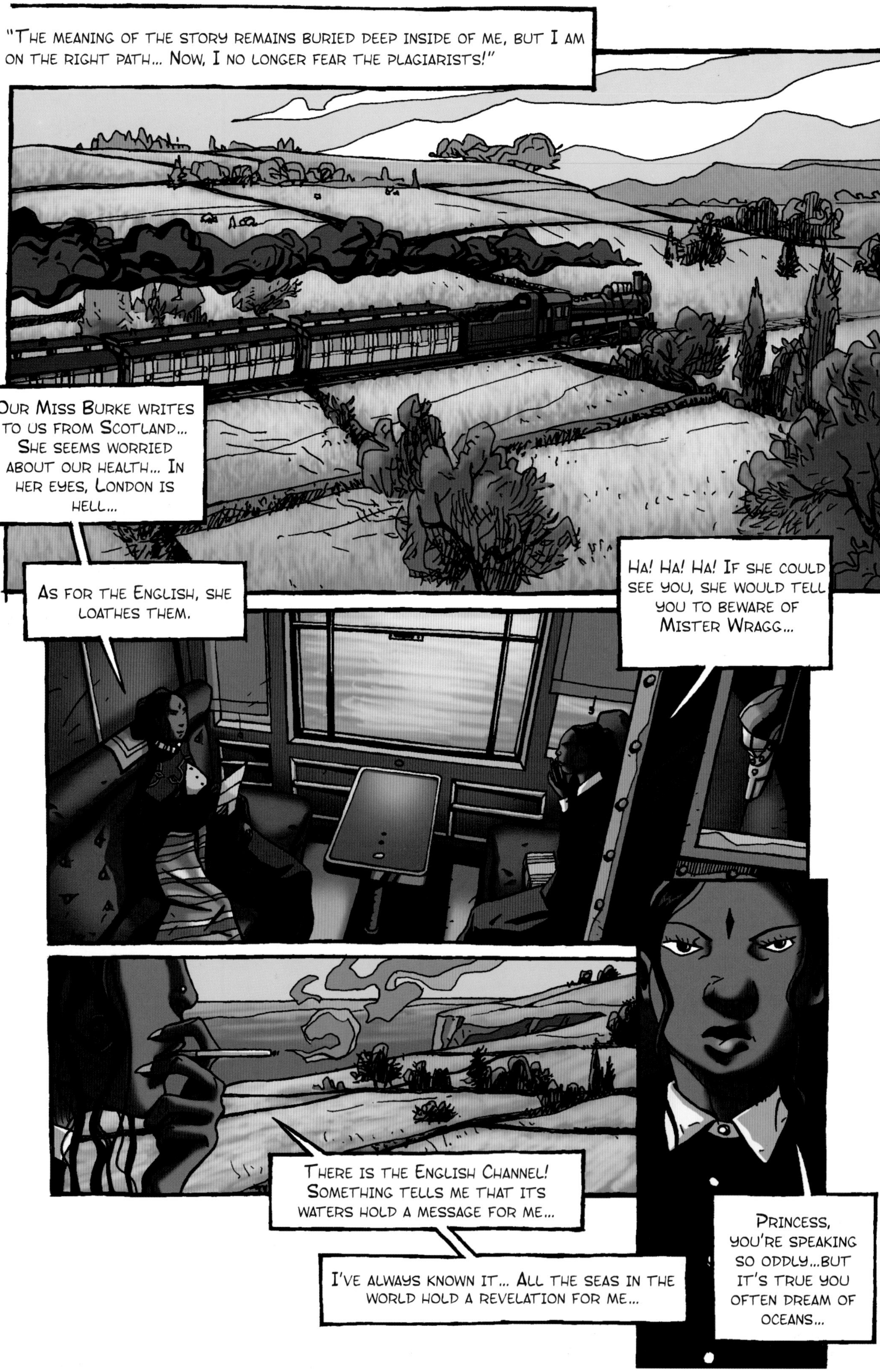
"The meaning of the story remains buried deep inside of me, but I am on the right path... Now, I no longer fear the plagiarists!"
Our Miss Burke writes to us from Scotland... She seems worried about our health... In her eyes, London is hell...
As for the English, she loathes them.
Ha! Ha! Ha! If she could see you, she would tell you to beware of Mister Wragg...
There is the English Channel! Something tells me that its waters hold a message for me...
I've always known it... All the seas in the world hold a revelation for me...
Princess, you're speaking so oddly...but it's true you often dream of oceans...

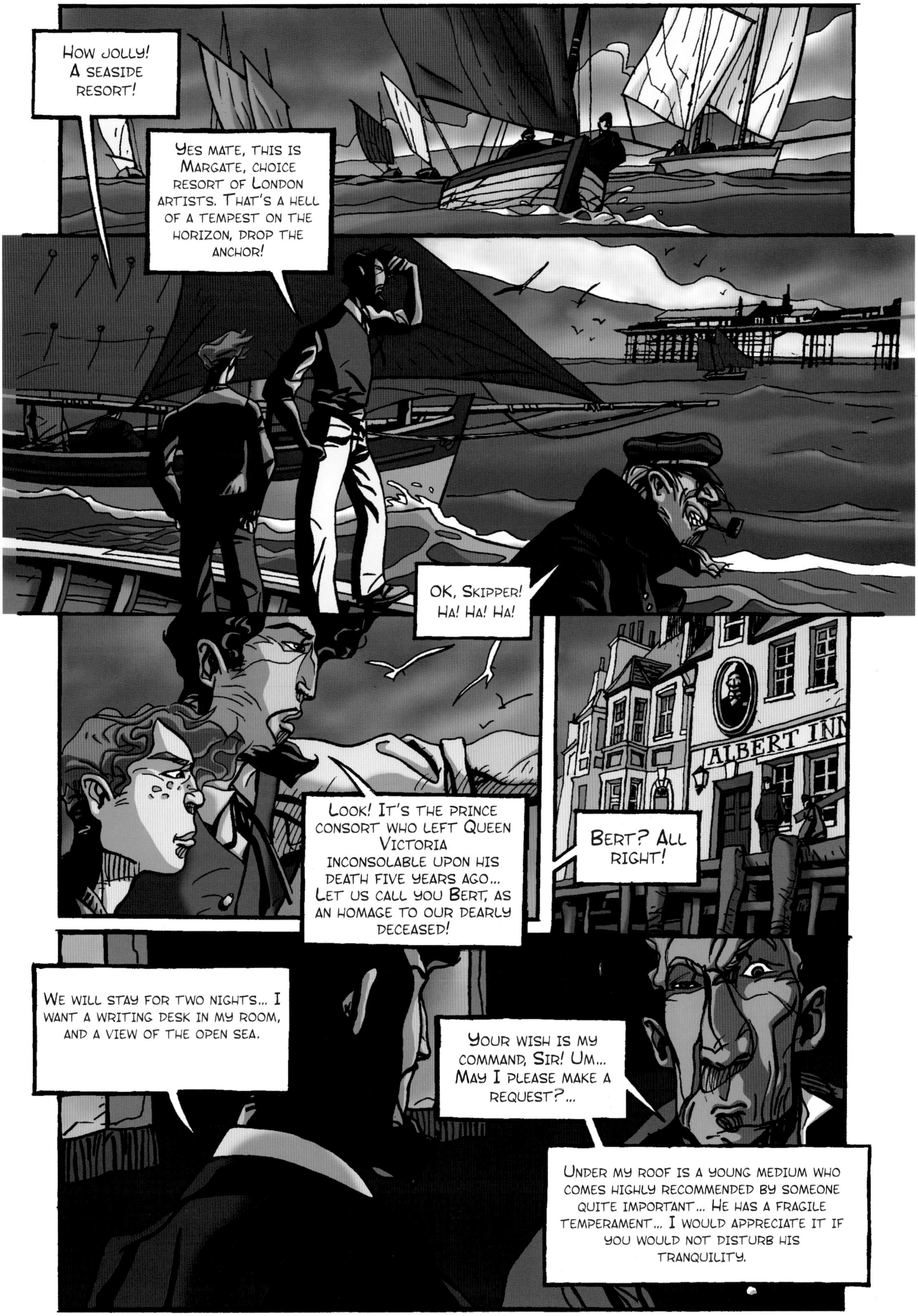

How jolly! A seaside resort!
Yes mate, this is Margate, choice resort of London artists. That's a hell of a tempest on the horizon, drop the anchor!
OK, Skipper! Ha! Ha! Ha!
Look! It's the prince consort who left Queen Victoria inconsolable upon his death five years ago... Let us call you Bert, as an homage to our dearly deceased!
ALBERT INN
Bert? All right!
We will stay for two nights... I want a writing desk in my room, and a view of the open sea.
Your wish is my command, Sir! Um... May I please make a request?...
Under my roof is a young medium who comes highly recommended by someone quite important... He has a fragile temperament... I would appreciate it if you would not disturb his tranquility.

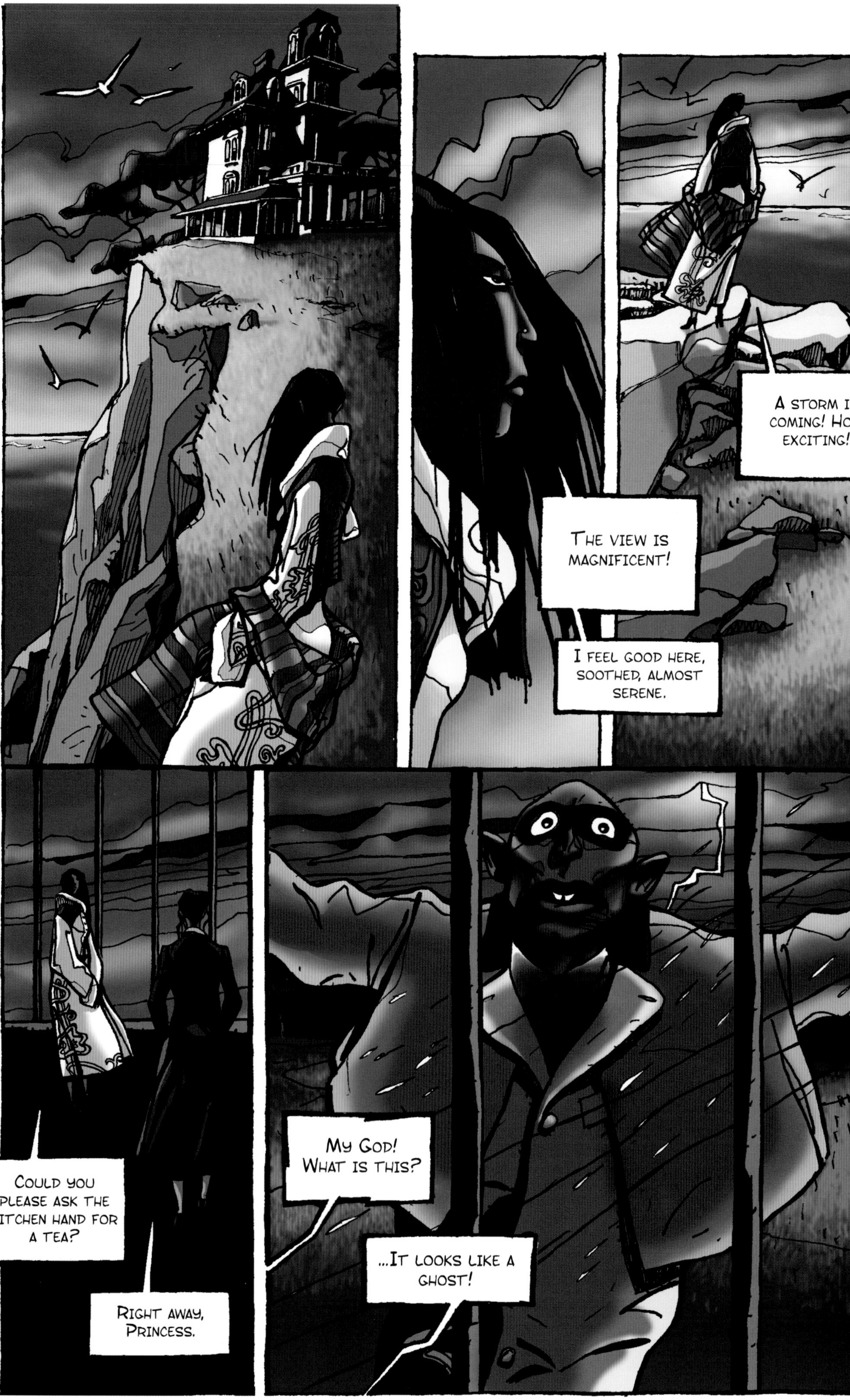
The view is magnificent!
I feel good here, soothed, almost serene.
A storm is coming! How exciting!
Could you please ask the kitchen hand for a tea?
Right away, Princess.
My God! What is this?
...It looks like a ghost!

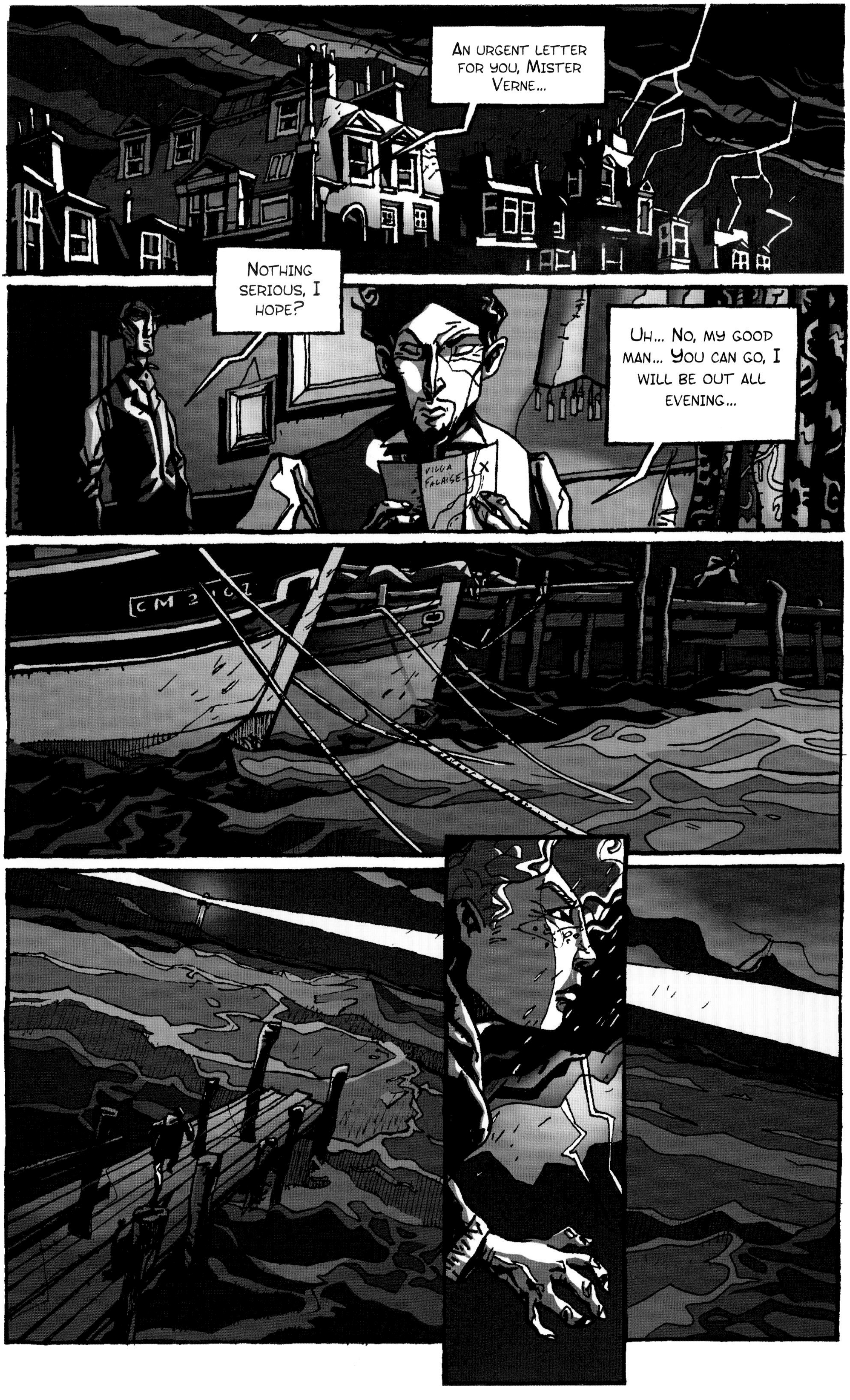
An urgent letter for you, Mister Verne...
Nothing serious, I hope?
Uh... No, my good man... You can go, I will be out all evening...
Villa Falaise

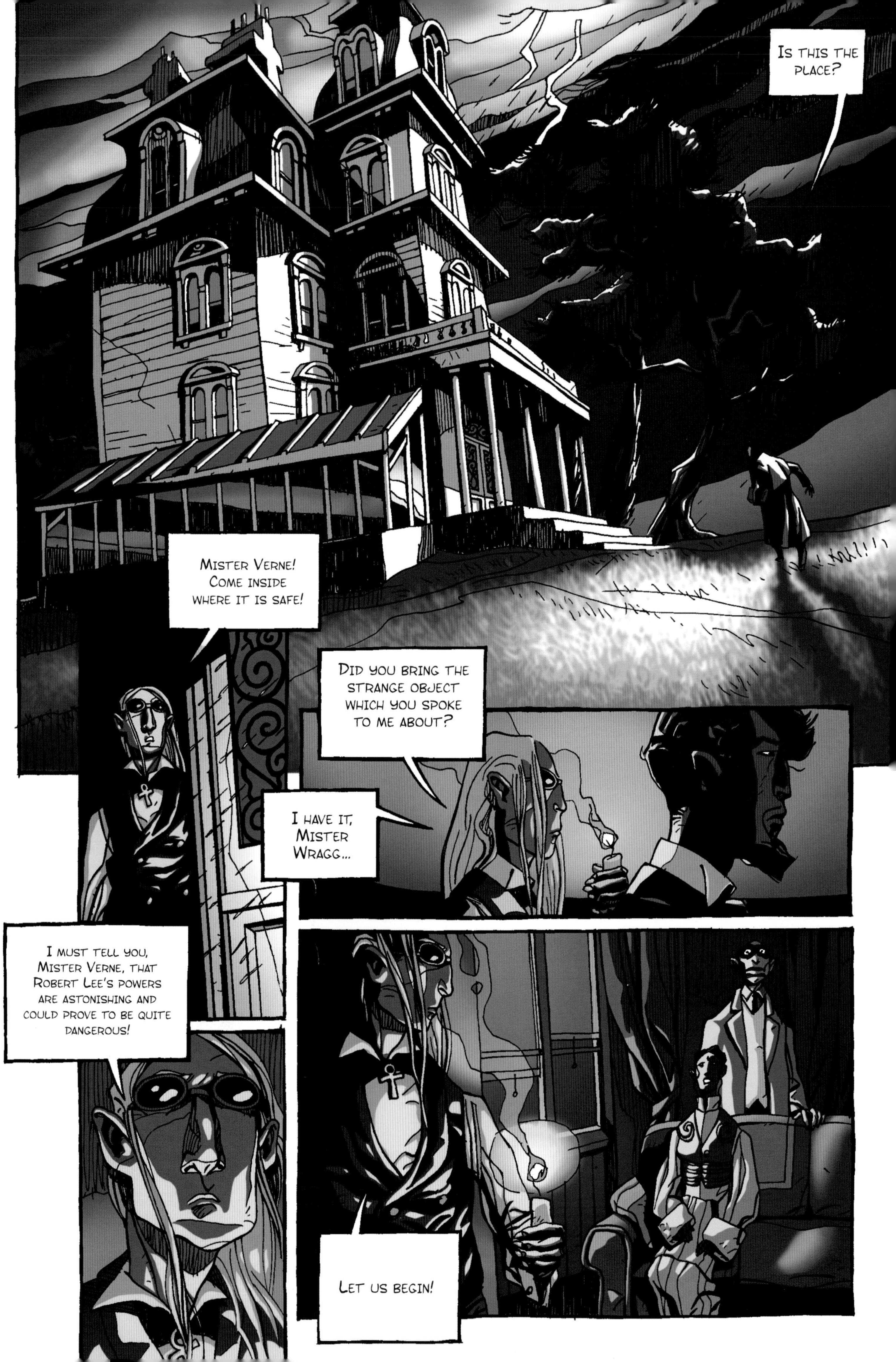
Is this the place?
Mister Verne! Come inside where it is safe!
Did you bring the strange object which you spoke to me about?
I have it, Mister Wragg...
I must tell you, Mister Verne, that Robert Lee's powers are astonishing and could prove to be quite dangerous!
Let us begin!

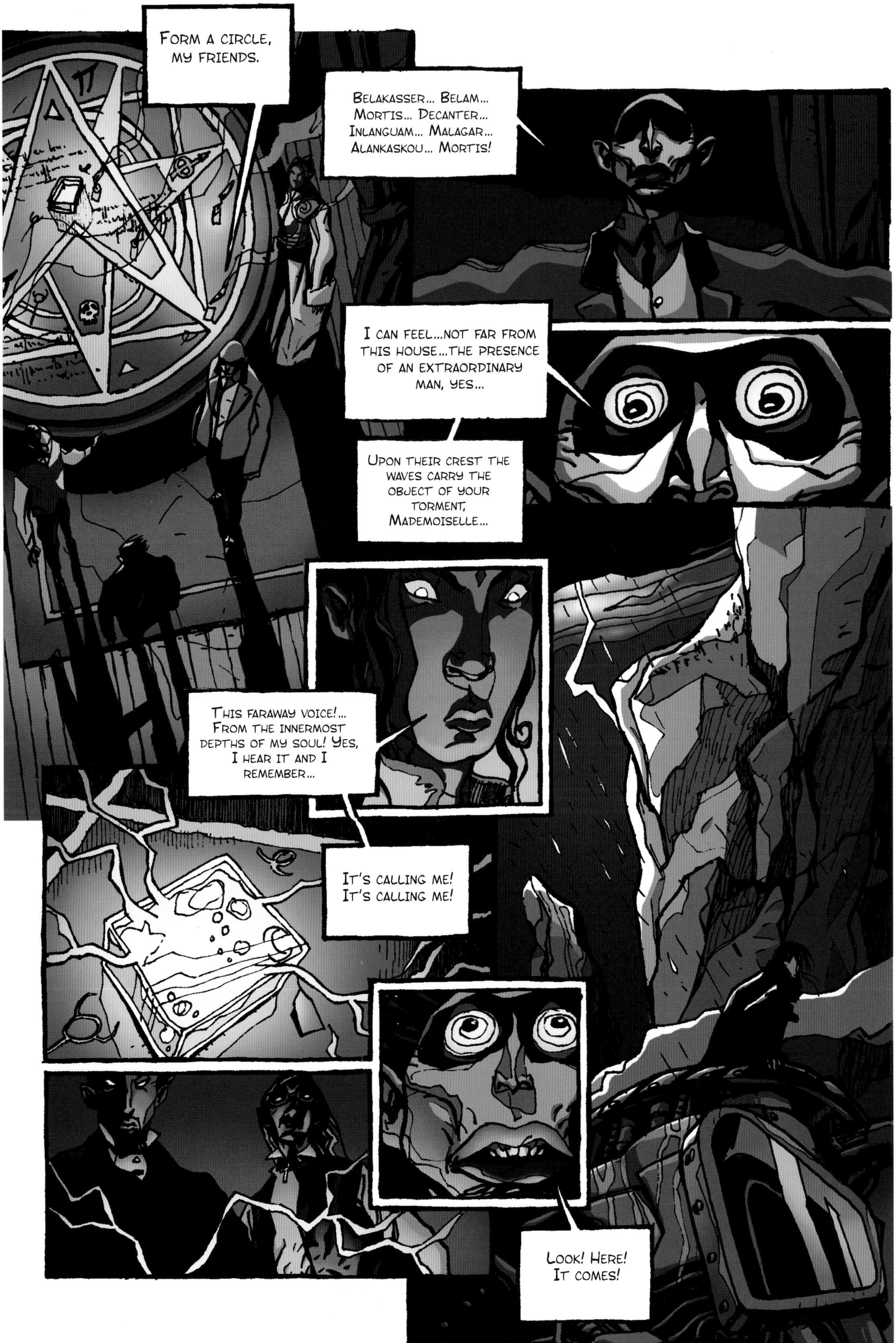
Form a circle, my friends.
Belakasser... Belam... Mortis... Decanter... Inlanguam... Malagar... Alankaskou... Mortis!
I can feel...not far from this house...the presence of an extraordinary man, yes...
Upon their crest the waves carry the object of your torment, Mademoiselle...
This faraway voice!... From the innermost depths of my soul! Yes, I hear it and I remember...
It's calling me! It's calling me!
Look! Here! It comes!

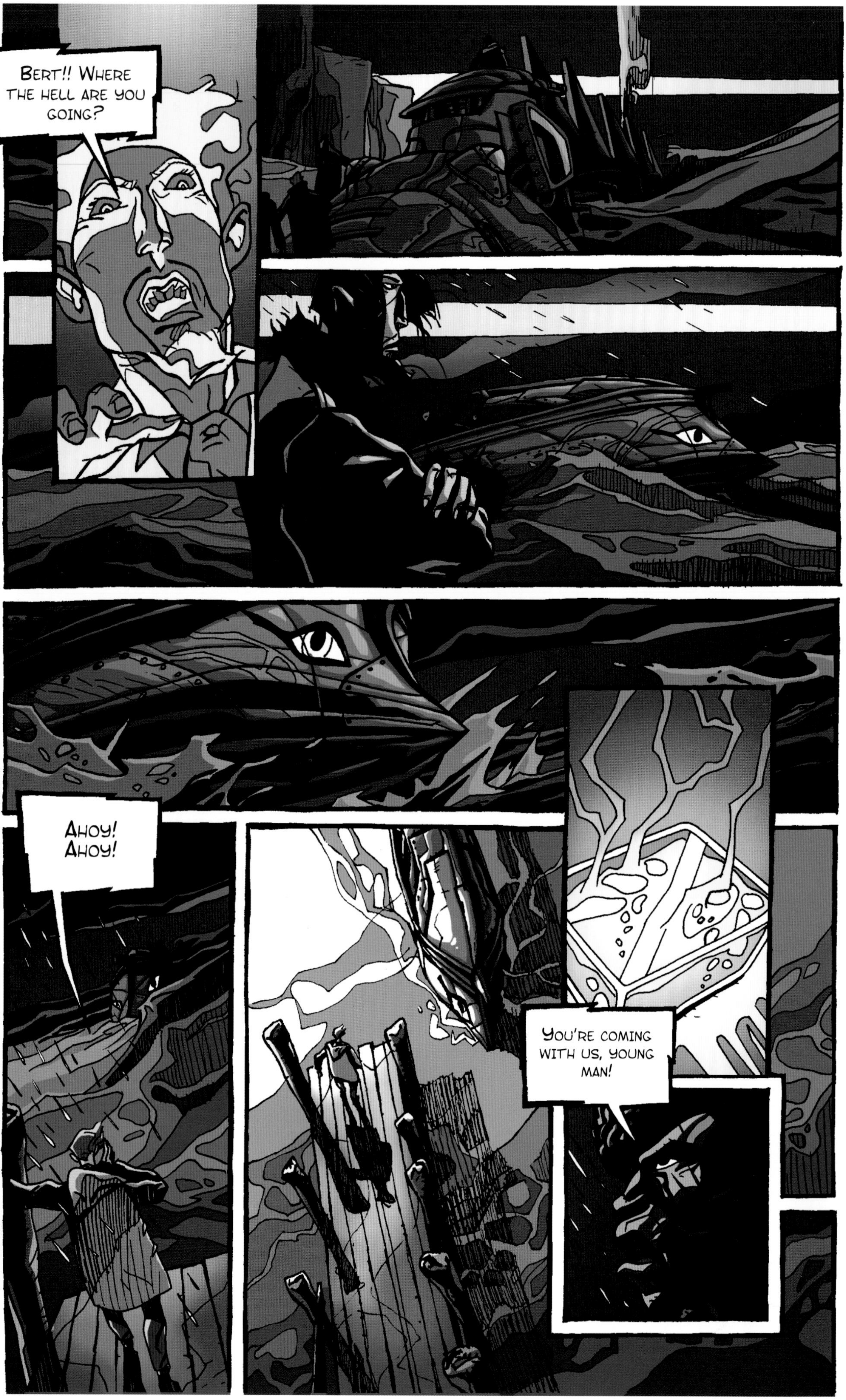

Bert!! Where the hell are you going?
Ahoy! Ahoy!
You're coming with us, young man!

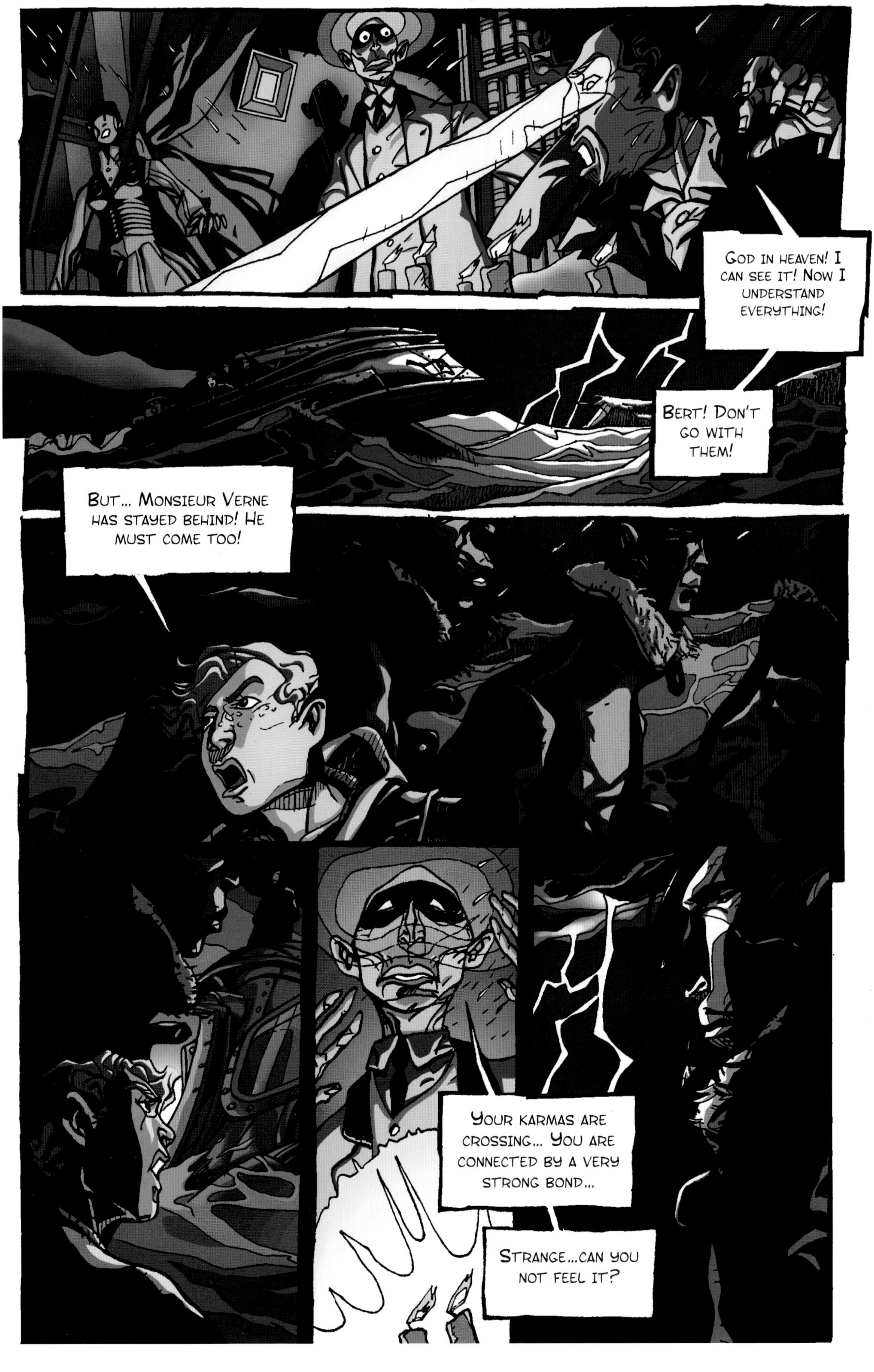

GOD IN HEAVEN! I CAN SEE IT! NOW I UNDERSTAND EVERYTHING!
BERT! DON'T GO WITH THEM!
BUT... MONSIEUR VERNE HAS STAYED BEHIND! HE MUST COME TOO!
YOUR KARMAS ARE CROSSING... YOU ARE CONNECTED BY A VERY STRONG BOND...
STRANGE...CAN YOU NOT FEEL IT?

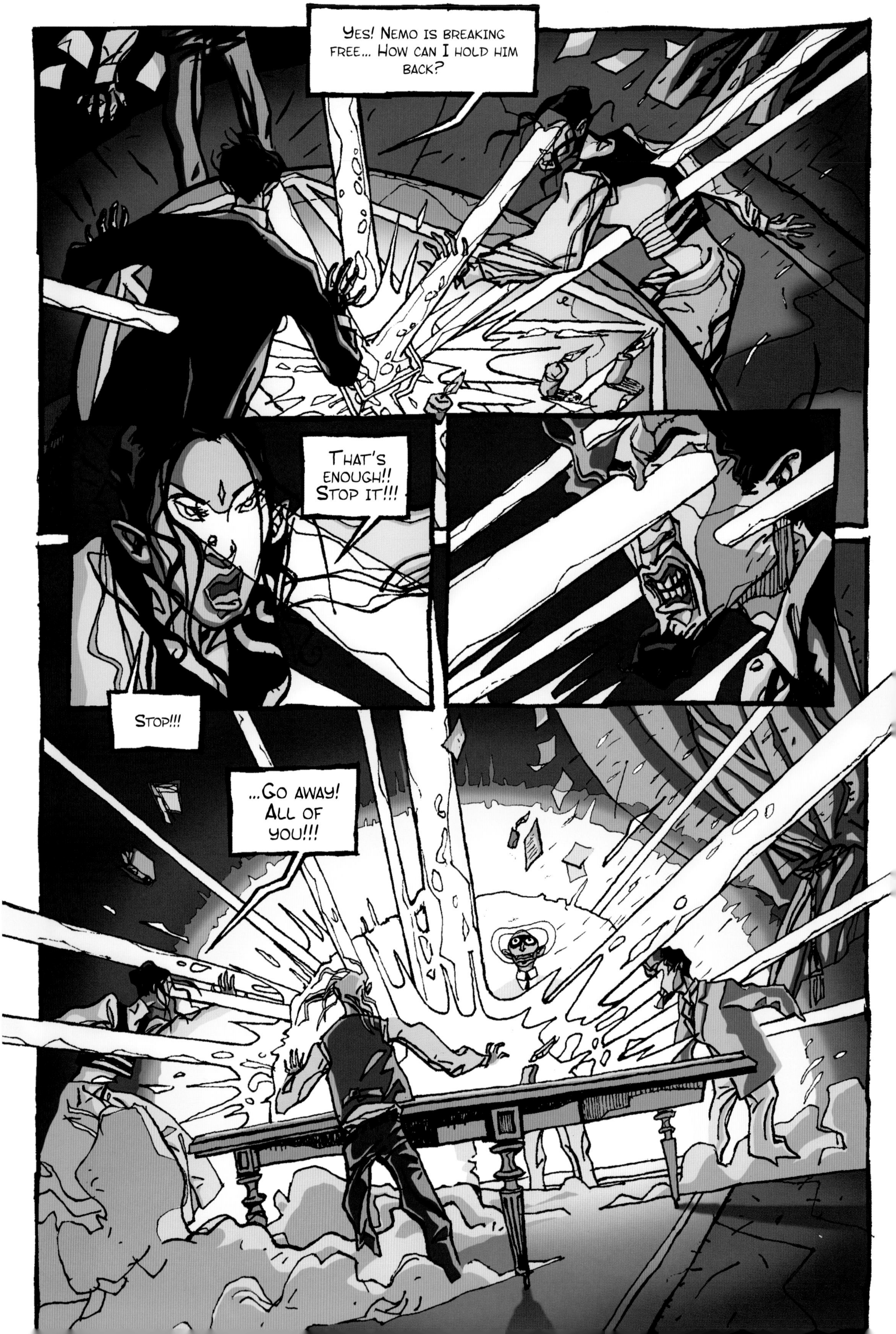

Yes! Nemo is breaking free... How can I hold him back?
That's enough!! Stop it!!!
Stop!!!
...Go away! All of you!!!

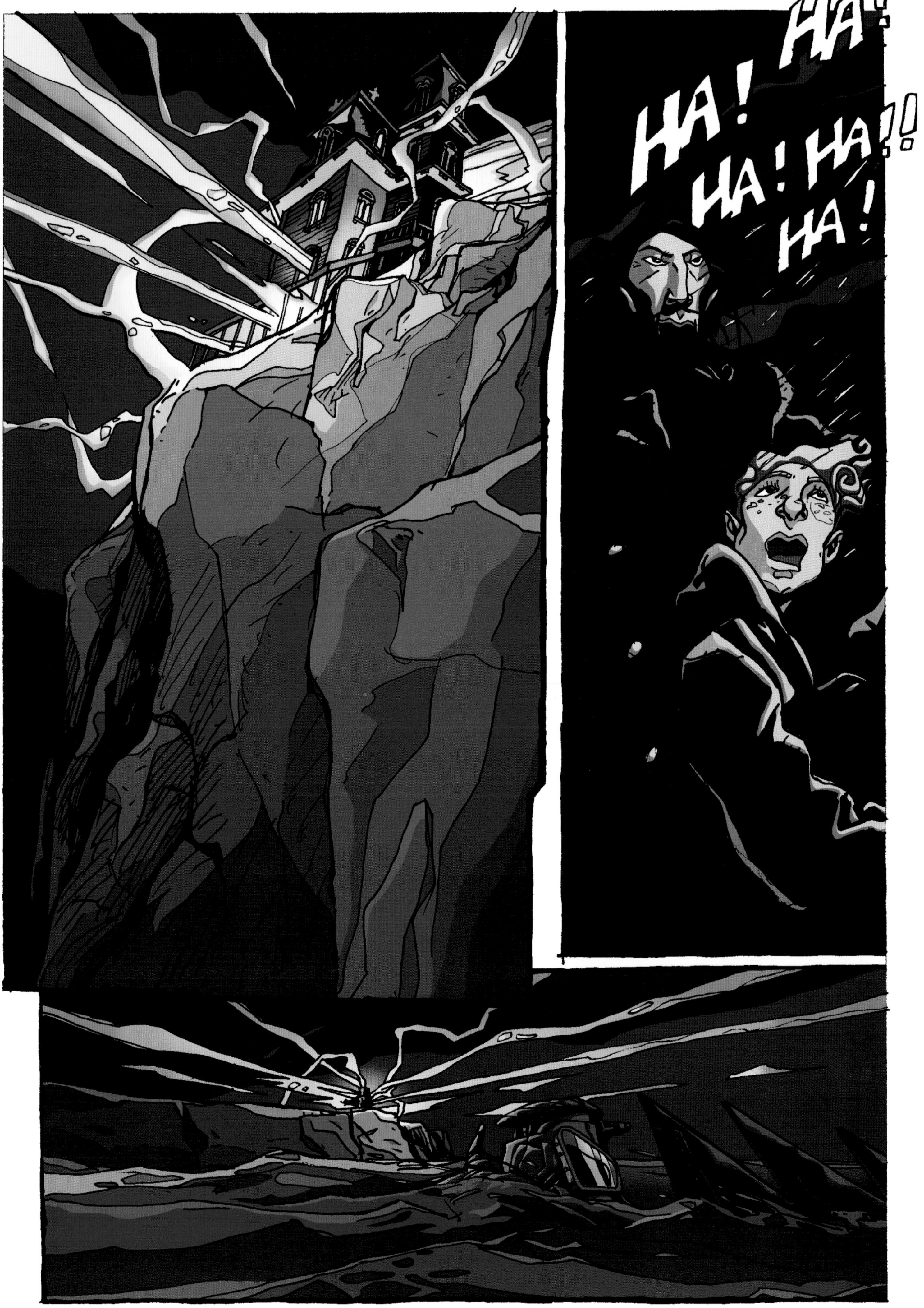
HA! HA!
HA! HA! HA!!
HA!

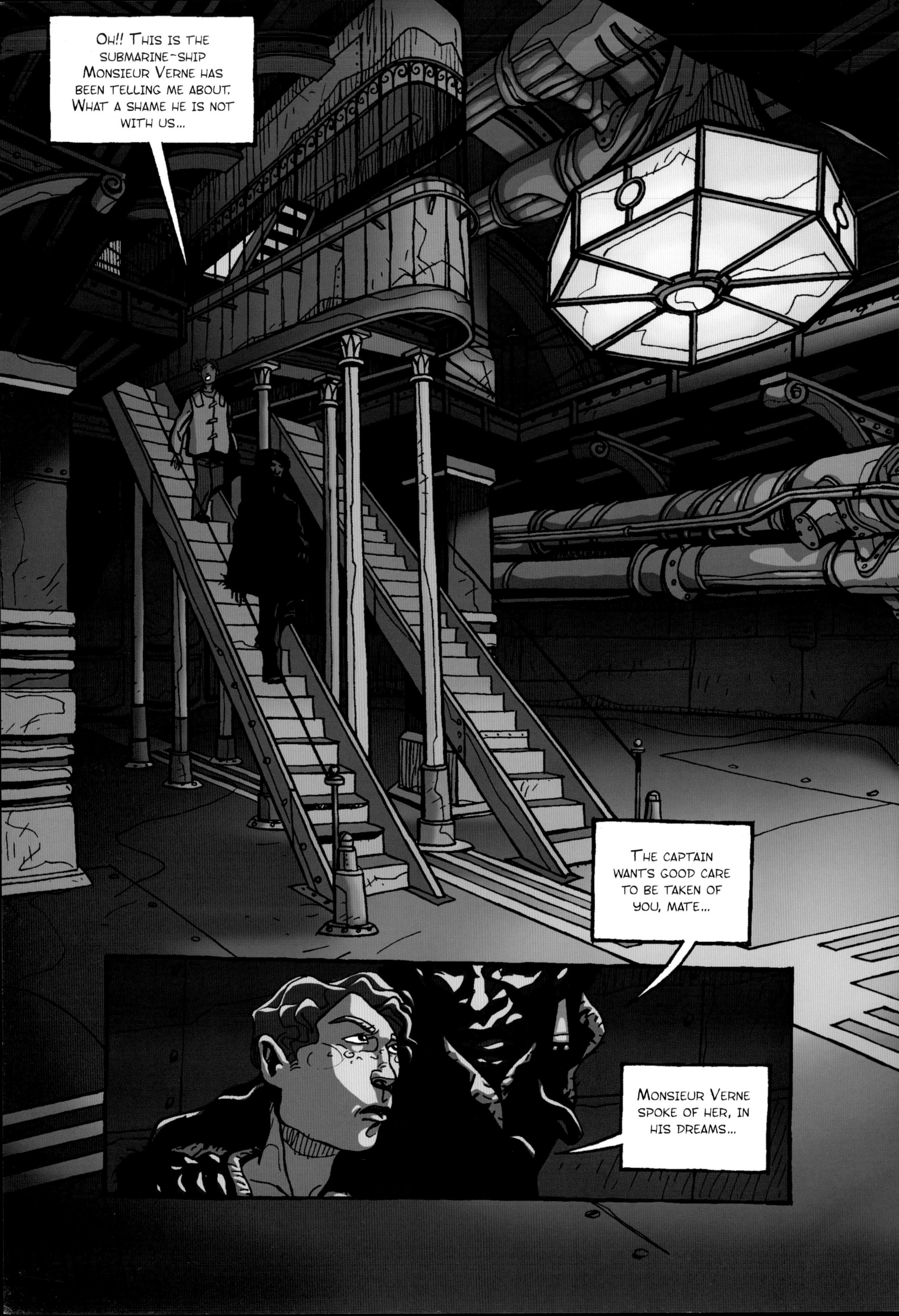

Oh!! This is the submarine-ship Monsieur Verne has been telling me about. What a shame he is not with us...
The captain wants good care to be taken of you, mate...
Monsieur Verne spoke of her, in his dreams...

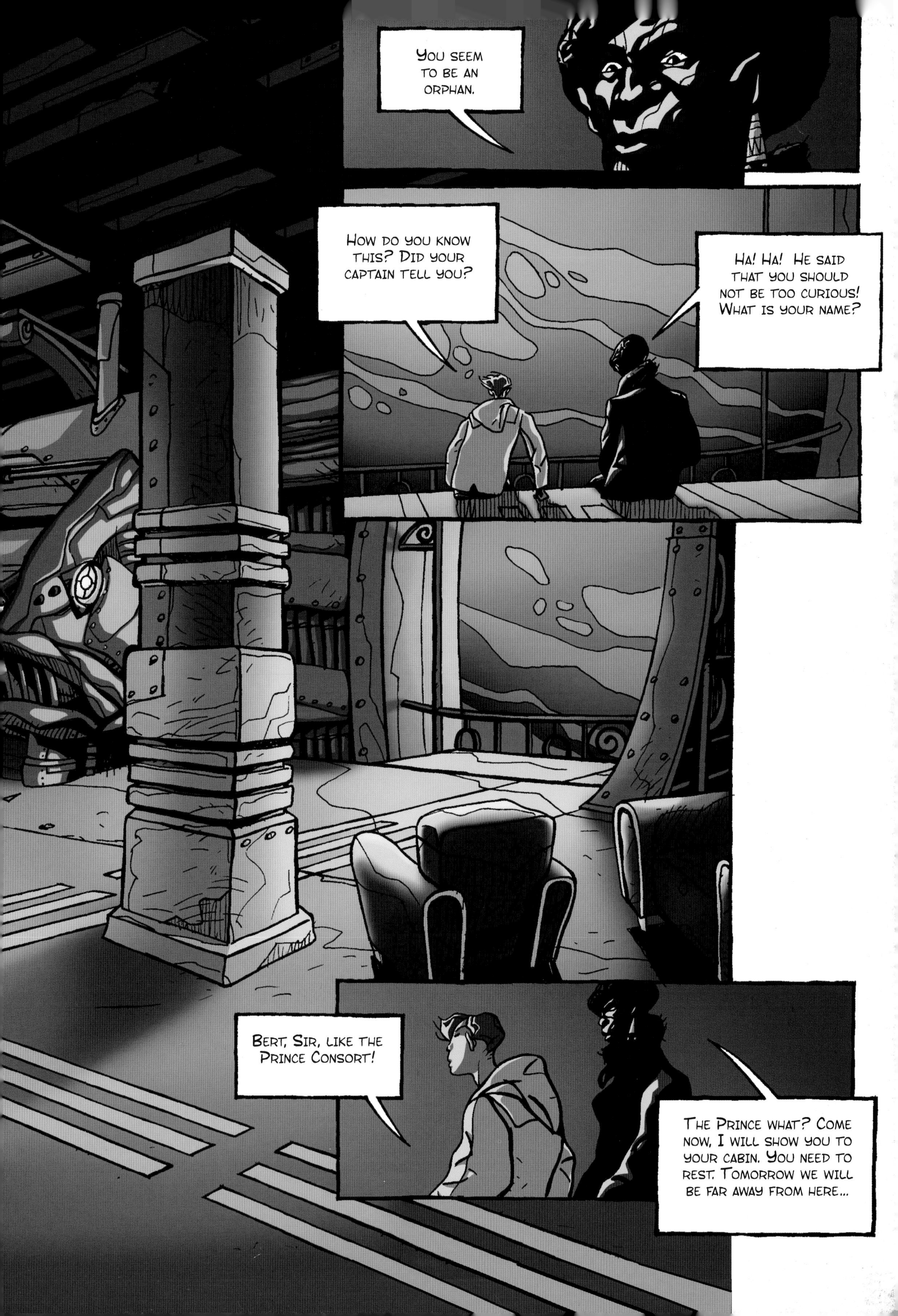
You seem to be an orphan.
How do you know this? Did your captain tell you?
Ha! Ha! He said that you should not be too curious! What is your name?
Bert, Sir, like the Prince Consort!
The Prince what? Come now, I will show you to your cabin. You need to rest. Tomorrow we will be far away from here...

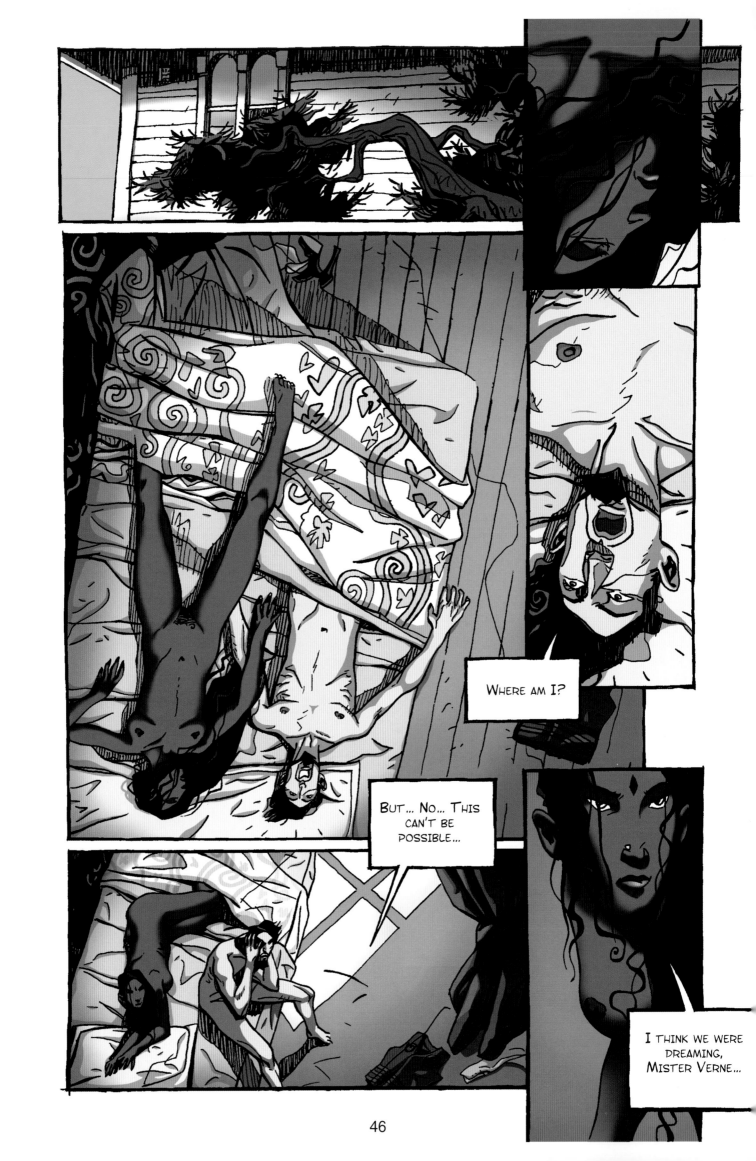

WHERE AM I?

BUT... NO... THIS CAN'T BE POSSIBLE...

I THINK WE WERE DREAMING, MISTER VERNE...

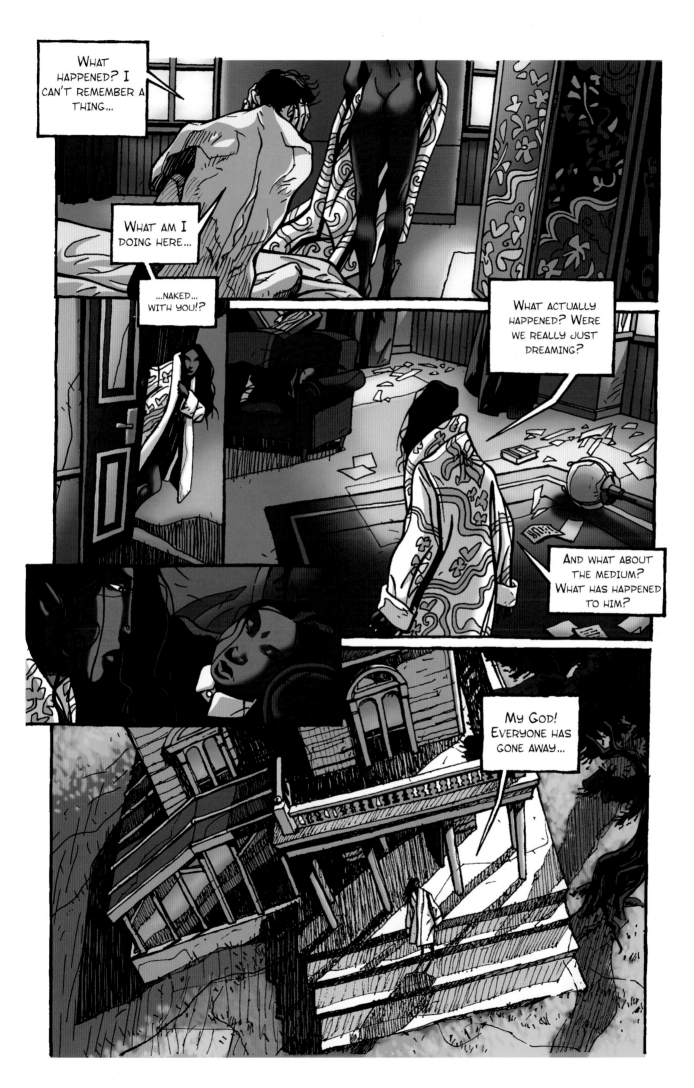

WHAT HAPPENED? I CAN'T REMEMBER A THING...

WHAT AM I DOING HERE...

...NAKED... WITH YOU!?

WHAT ACTUALLY HAPPENED? WERE WE REALLY JUST DREAMING?

AND WHAT ABOUT THE MEDIUM? WHAT HAS HAPPENED TO HIM?

MY GOD! EVERYONE HAS GONE AWAY...

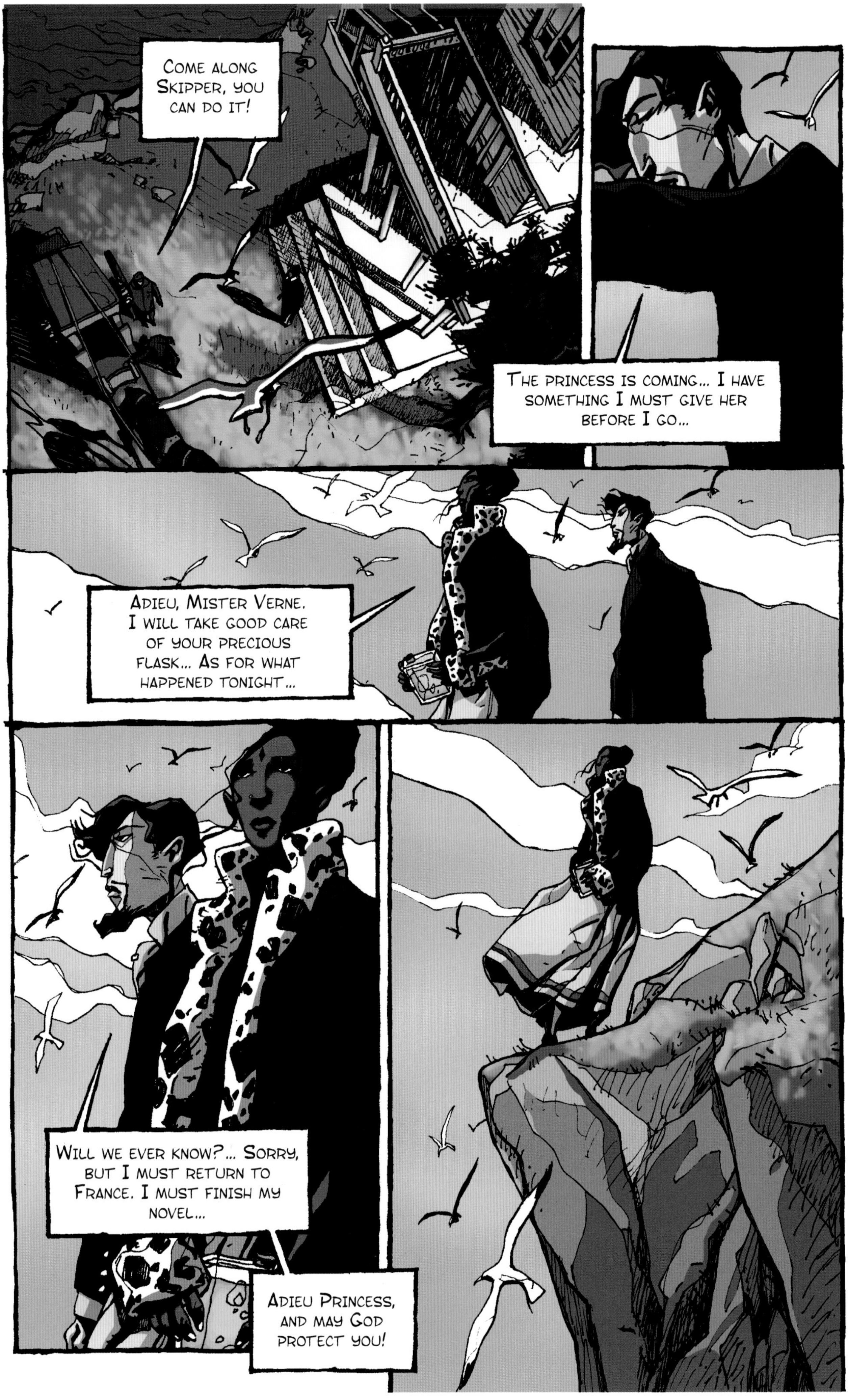

Come along Skipper, you can do it!
The princess is coming... I have something I must give her before I go...
Adieu, Mister Verne. I will take good care of your precious flask... As for what happened tonight...
Will we ever know?... Sorry, but I must return to France. I must finish my novel...
Adieu Princess, and may God protect you!

READING ROOM OF THE BRITISH MUSEUM...

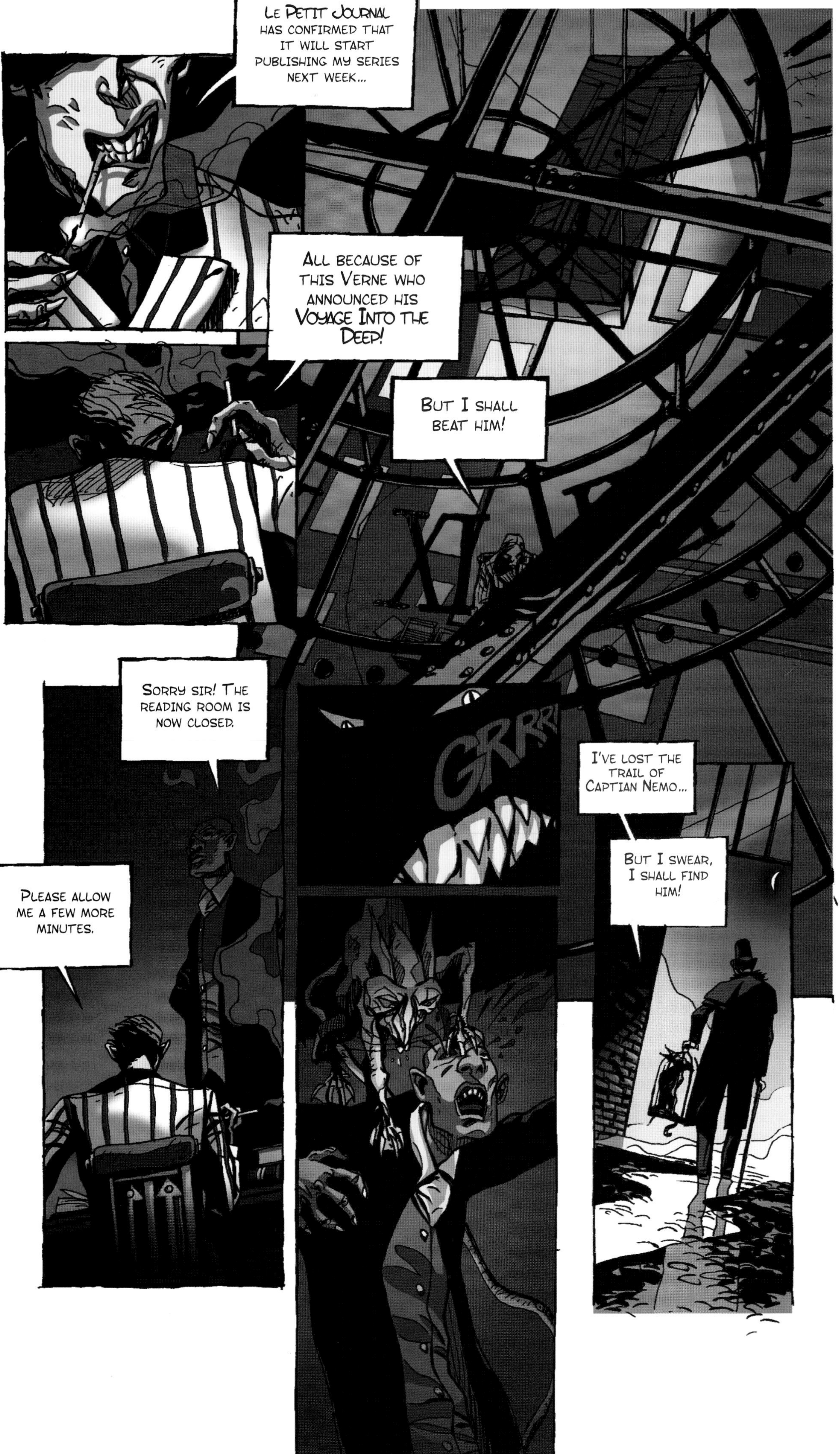
Le Petit Journal has confirmed that it will start publishing my series next week...
All because of this Verne who announced his Voyage Into the Deep!
But I shall beat him!
Sorry sir! The reading room is now closed.
Please allow me a few more minutes.
GRRR
I've lost the trail of Captian Nemo...
But I swear, I shall find him!

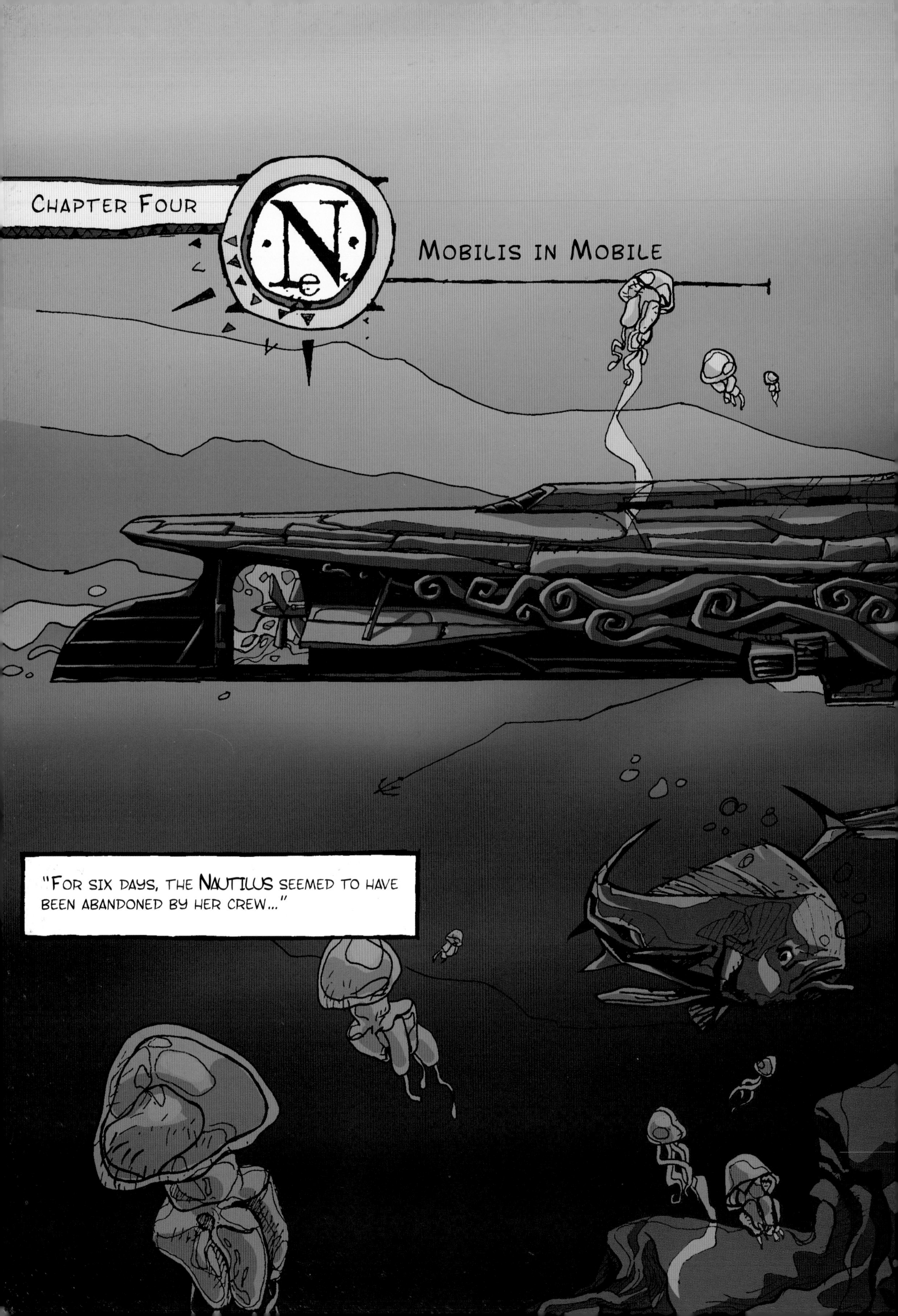
CHAPTER FOUR
Ne
MOBILIS IN MOBILE
"FOR SIX DAYS, THE NAUTILUS SEEMED TO HAVE BEEN ABANDONED BY HER CREW..."

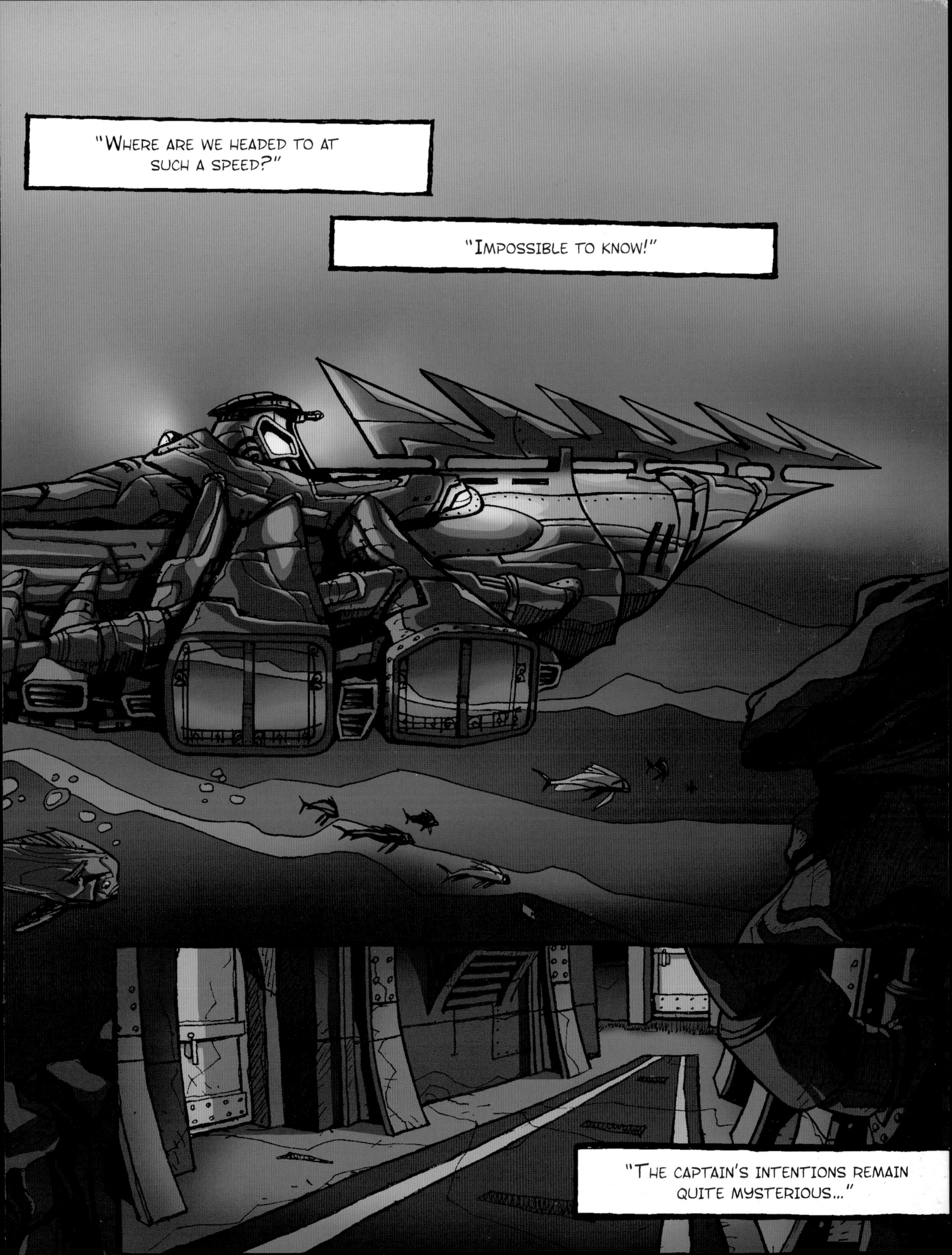
"Where are we headed to at such a speed?"
"Impossible to know!"
"The captain's intentions remain quite mysterious..."

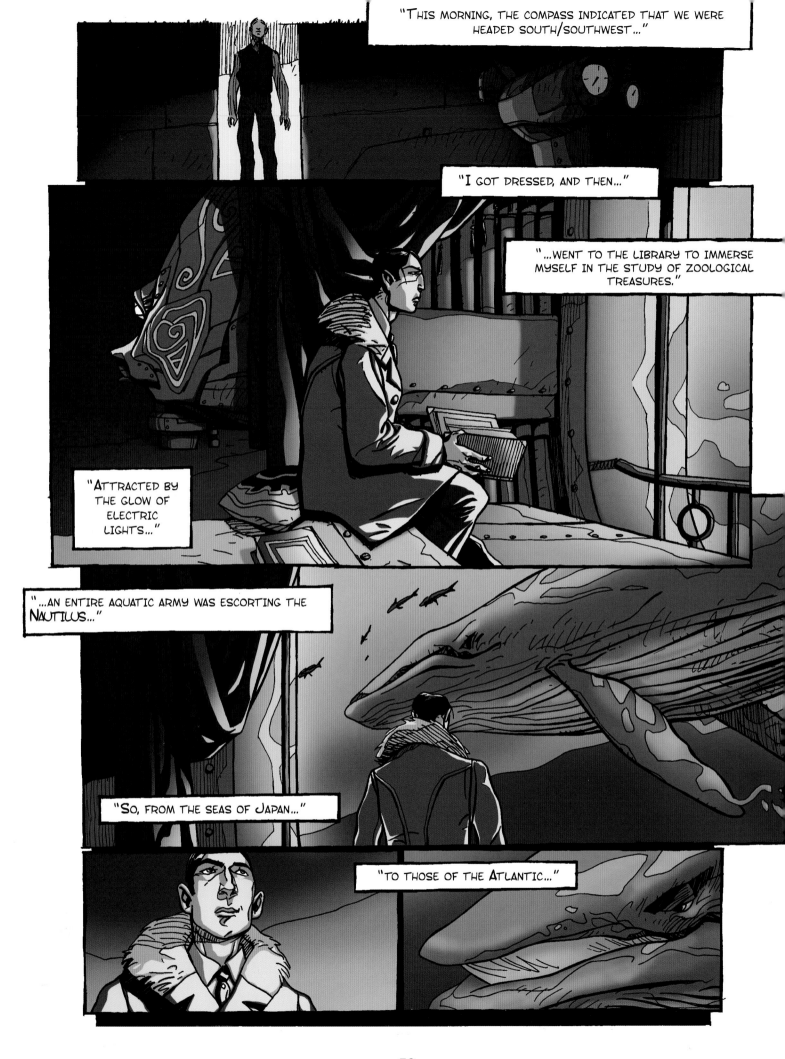

"THIS MORNING, THE COMPASS INDICATED THAT WE WERE HEADED SOUTH/SOUTHWEST..."

"I GOT DRESSED, AND THEN..."

"...WENT TO THE LIBRARY TO IMMERSE MYSELF IN THE STUDY OF ZOOLOGICAL TREASURES."

"ATTRACTED BY THE GLOW OF ELECTRIC LIGHTS..."

"...AN ENTIRE AQUATIC ARMY WAS ESCORTING THE NAUTILUS..."

"SO, FROM THE SEAS OF JAPAN..."

"TO THOSE OF THE ATLANTIC..."

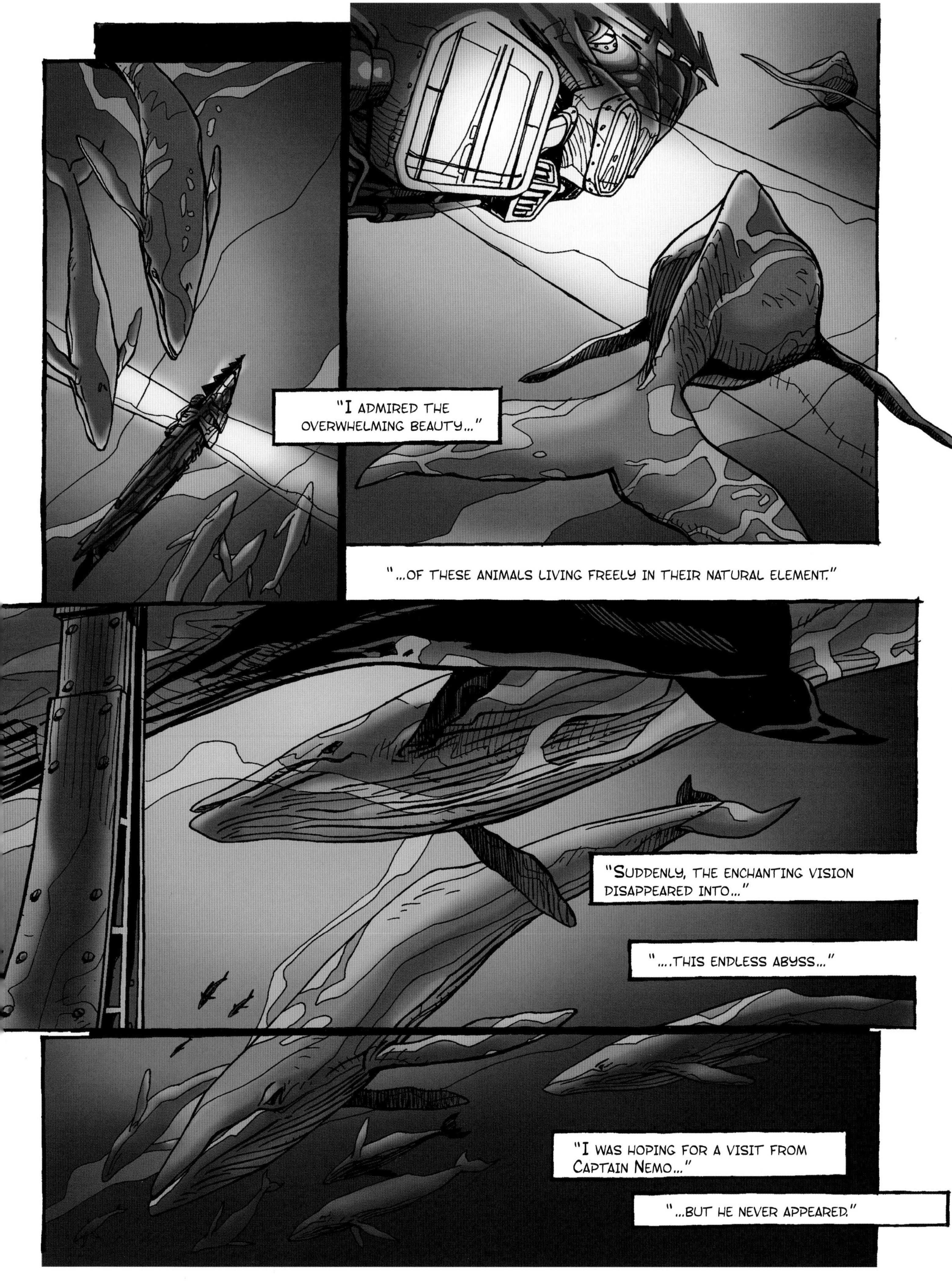
"I ADMIRED THE OVERWHELMING BEAUTY..."
"...OF THESE ANIMALS LIVING FREELY IN THEIR NATURAL ELEMENT."
"SUDDENLY, THE ENCHANTING VISION DISAPPEARED INTO..."
"....THIS ENDLESS ABYSS..."
"I WAS HOPING FOR A VISIT FROM CAPTAIN NEMO..."
"...BUT HE NEVER APPEARED."

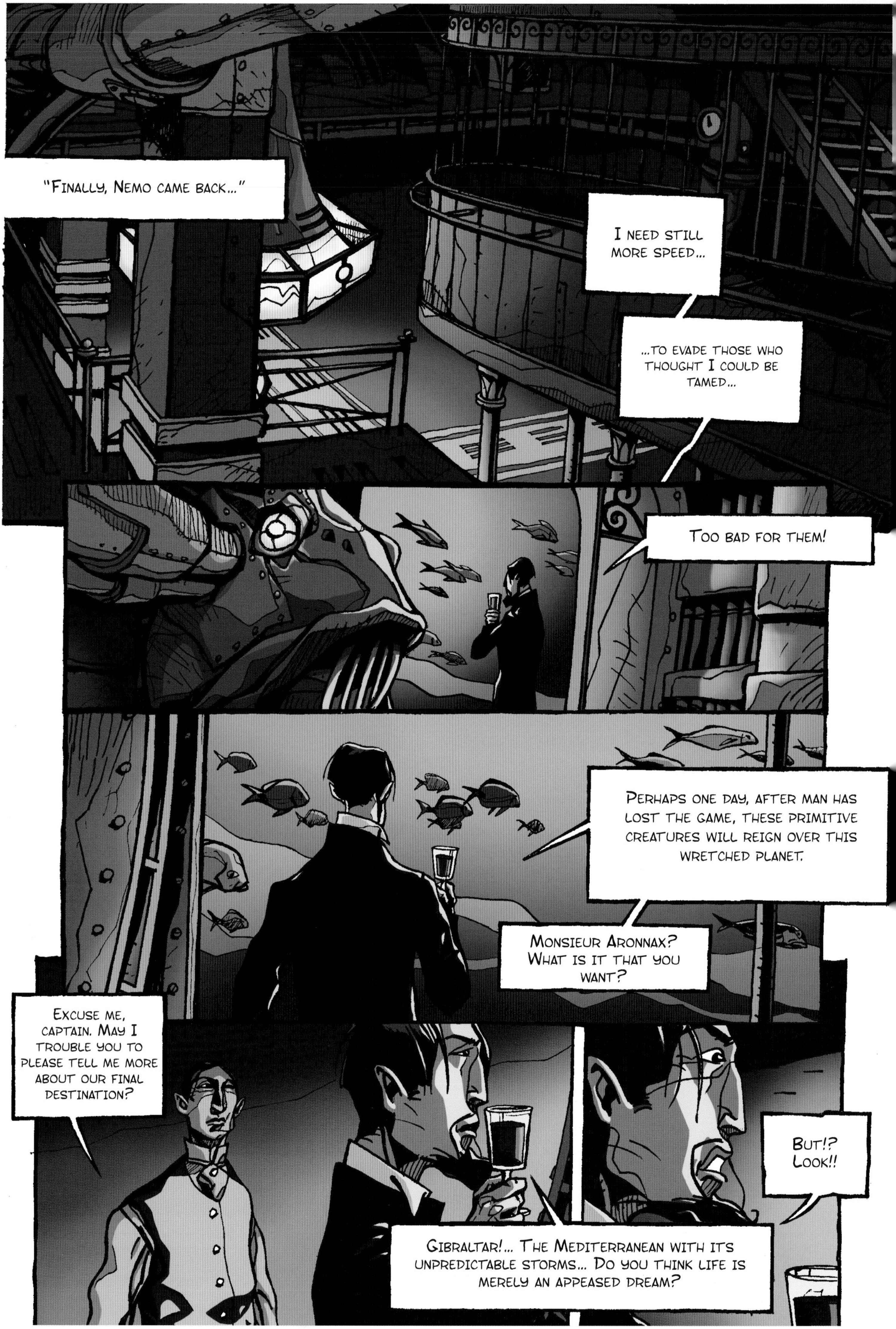
"Finally, Nemo came back..."
I need still more speed...
...to evade those who thought I could be tamed...
Too bad for them!
Perhaps one day, after man has lost the game, these primitive creatures will reign over this wretched planet.
Monsieur Aronnax? What is it that you want?
Excuse me, captain. May I trouble you to please tell me more about our final destination?
Gibraltar!... The Mediterranean with its unpredictable storms... Do you think life is merely an appeased dream?
But!? Look!!

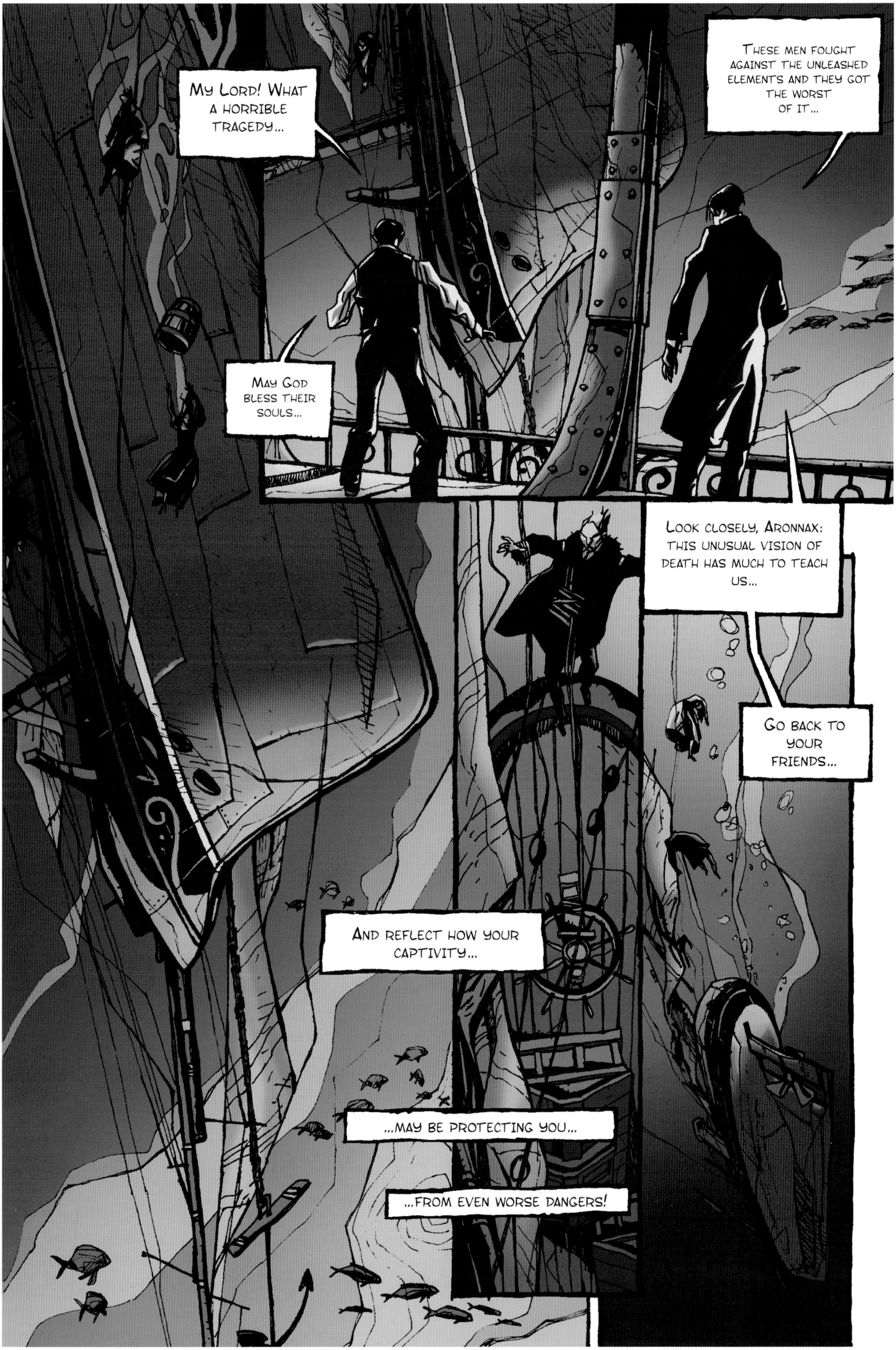
My Lord! What a horrible tragedy...
These men fought against the unleashed elements and they got the worst of it...
May God bless their souls...
Look closely, Aronnax: this unusual vision of death has much to teach us...
Go back to your friends...
And reflect how your captivity...
...may be protecting you...
...from even worse dangers!

"DAYS WENT BY..."

HAS HE TOLD YOU WHEN WE WILL SURFACE? I'M DYING OF INERTIA DOWN HERE!

NO, MY DEAR NED...ONLY GOD KNOWS... OR NOT...

MONSIEUR ARONNAX!! THE CAPTAIN IS WAITING FOR YOU ON THE BRIDGE...

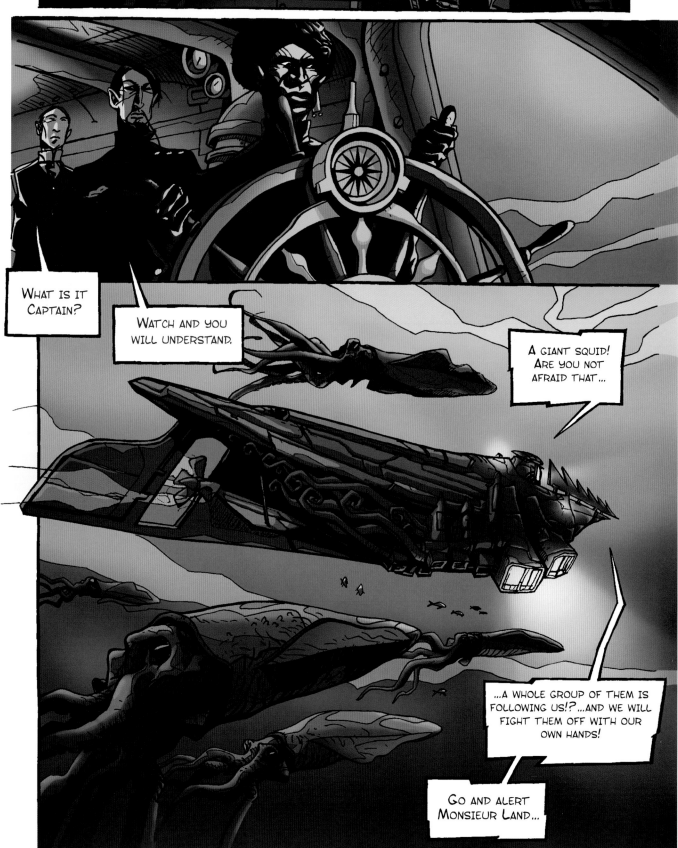

WHAT IS IT CAPTAIN?

WATCH AND YOU WILL UNDERSTAND.

A GIANT SQUID! ARE YOU NOT AFRAID THAT...

...A WHOLE GROUP OF THEM IS FOLLOWING US!?...AND WE WILL FIGHT THEM OFF WITH OUR OWN HANDS!

GO AND ALERT MONSIEUR LAND...

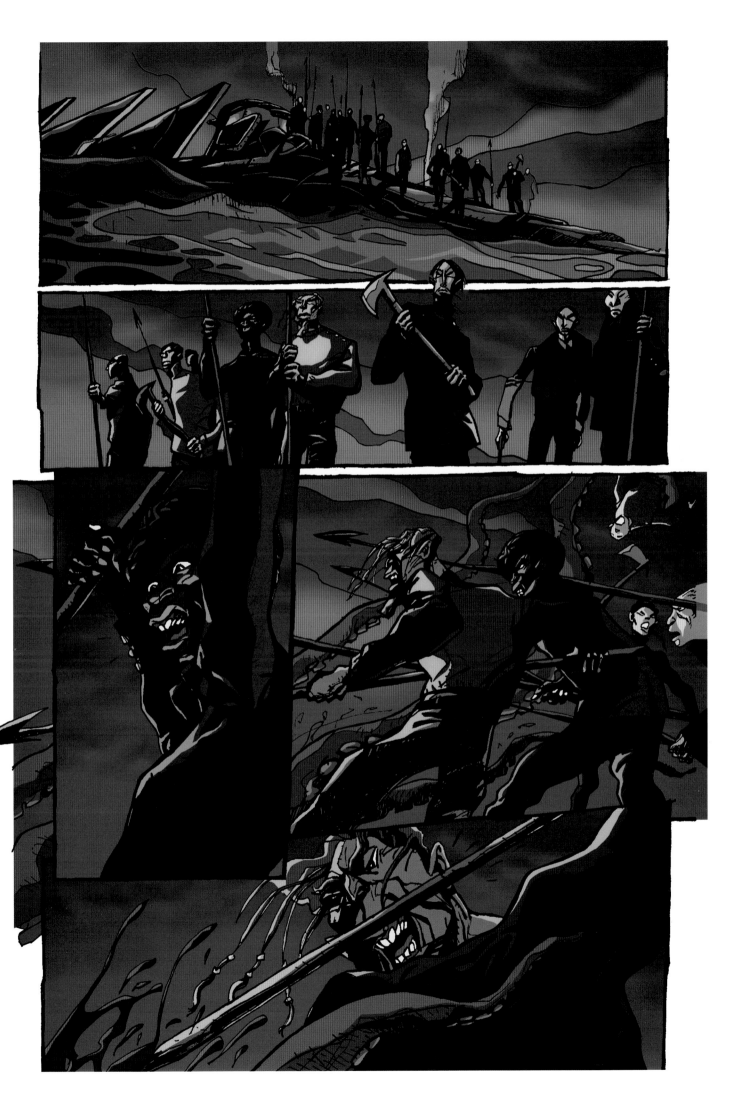

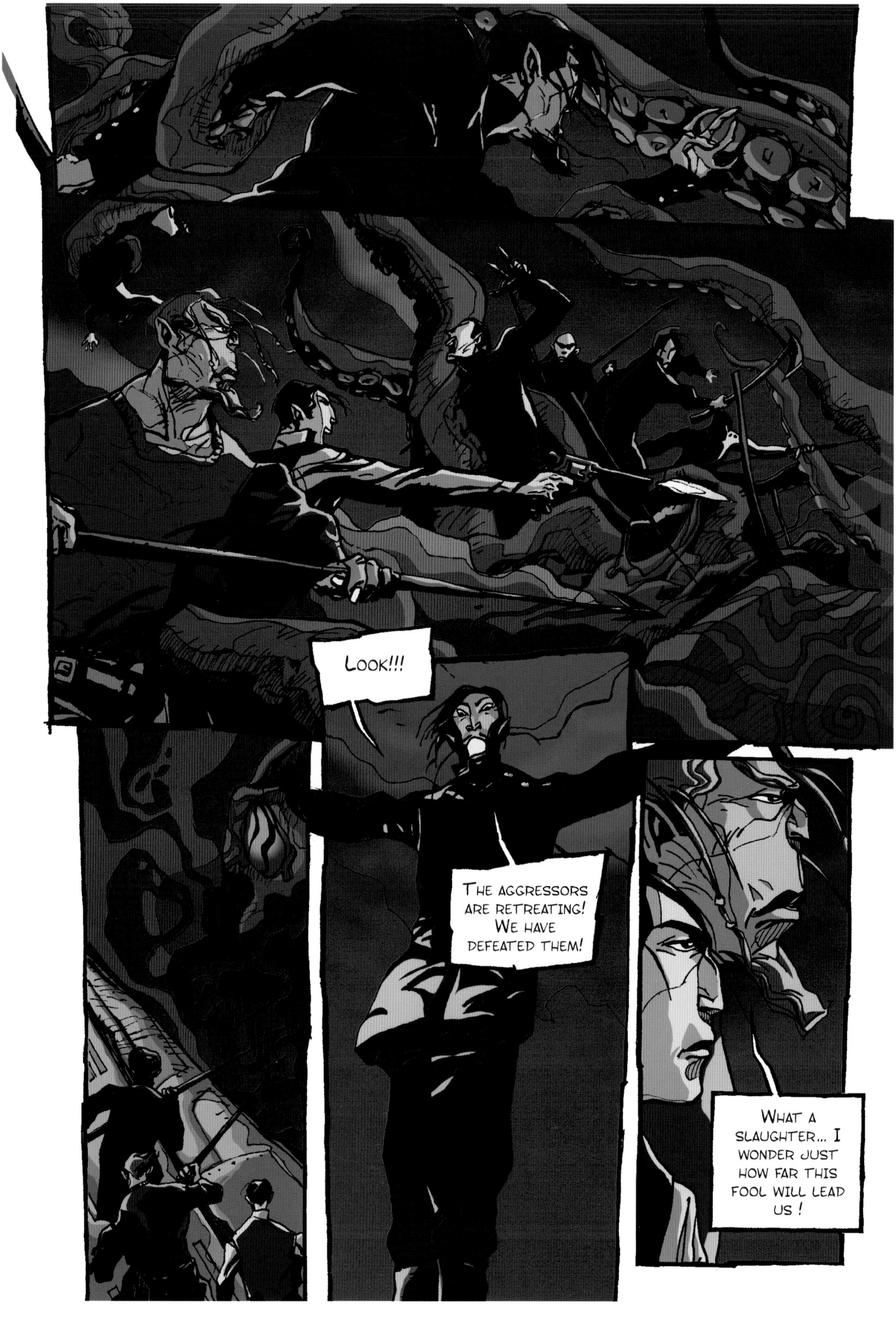
Look!!!
The aggressors are retreating! We have defeated them!
What a slaughter... I wonder just how far this fool will lead us !

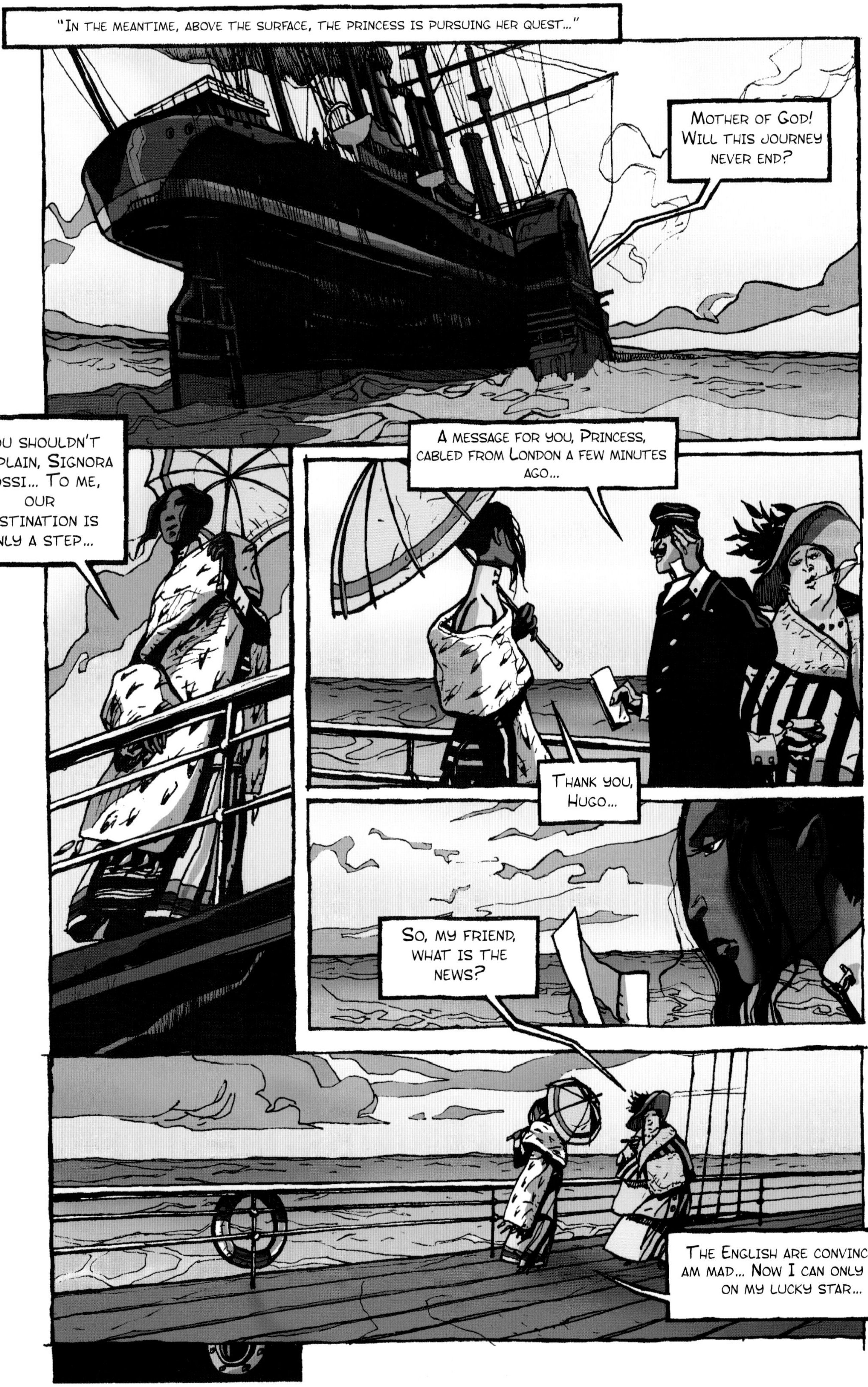
"In the meantime, above the surface, the princess is pursuing her quest..."
Mother of God! Will this journey never end?
You shouldn't complain, Signora Rossi... To me, our destination is only a step...
A message for you, Princess, cabled from London a few minutes ago...
Thank you, Hugo...
So, my friend, what is the news?
The English are convinced I am mad... Now I can only rely on my lucky star...

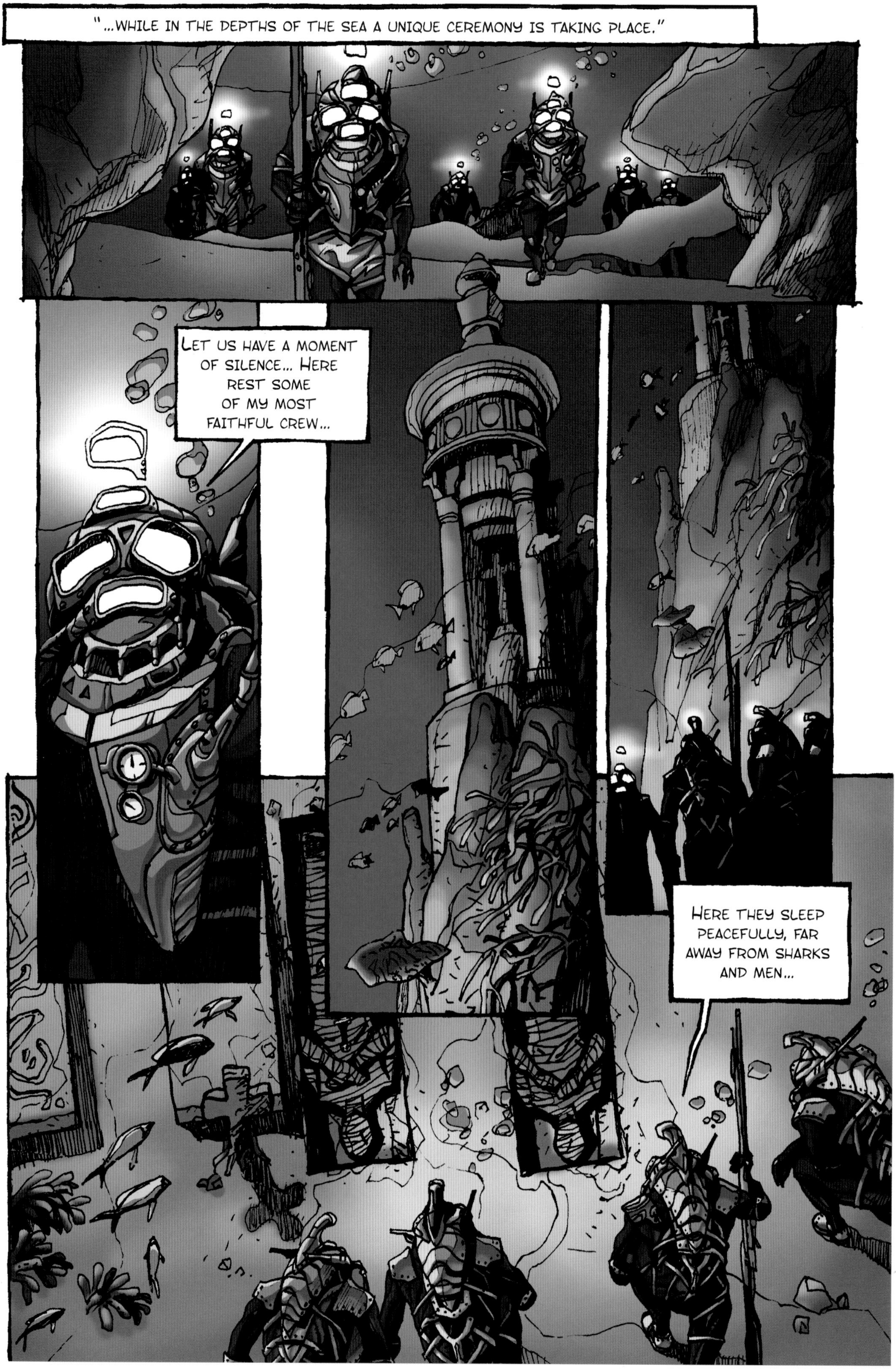
"...WHILE IN THE DEPTHS OF THE SEA A UNIQUE CEREMONY IS TAKING PLACE."
LET US HAVE A MOMENT OF SILENCE... HERE REST SOME OF MY MOST FAITHFUL CREW...
HERE THEY SLEEP PEACEFULLY, FAR AWAY FROM SHARKS AND MEN...

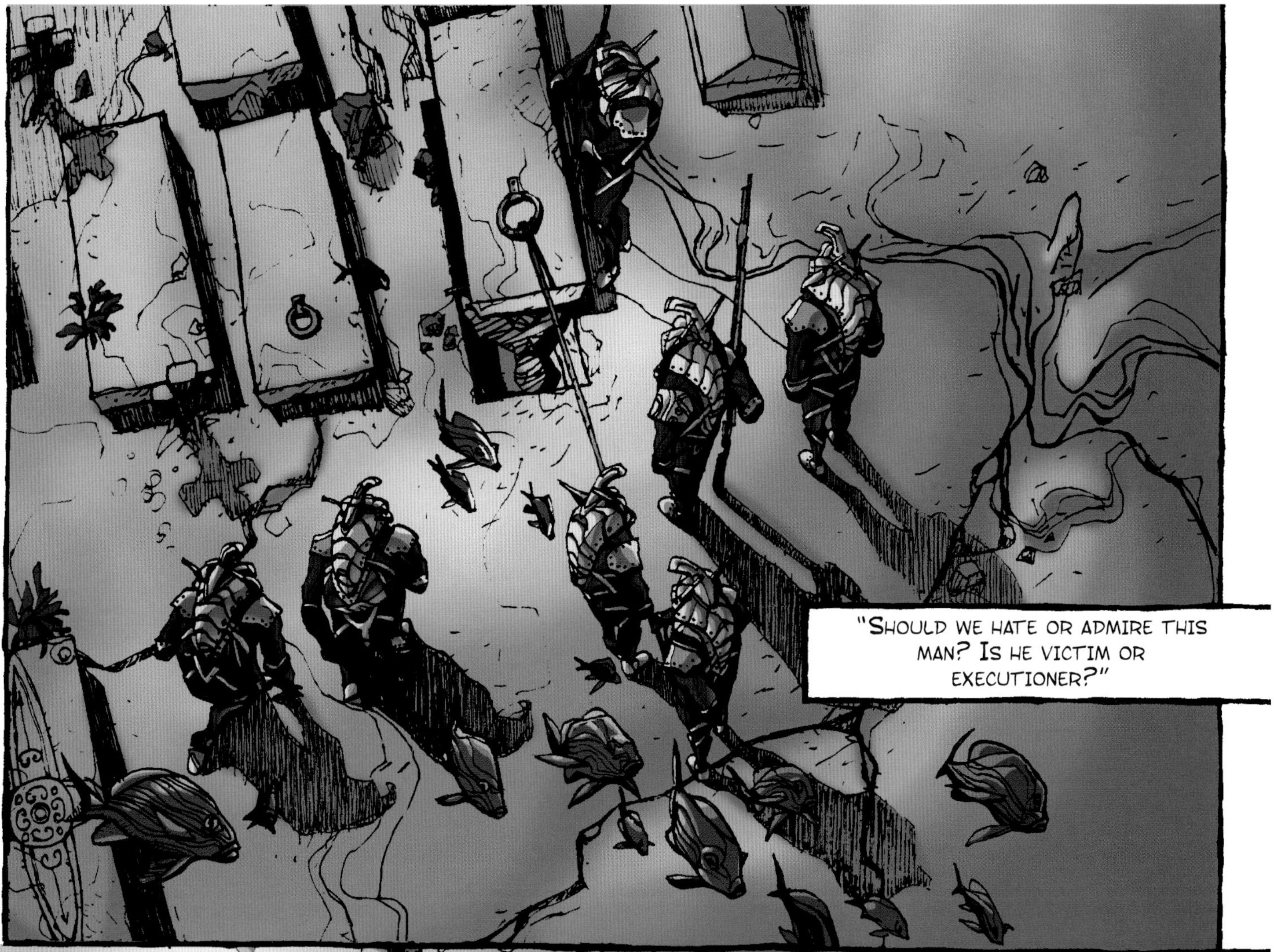
"Should we hate or admire this man? Is he victim or executioner?"
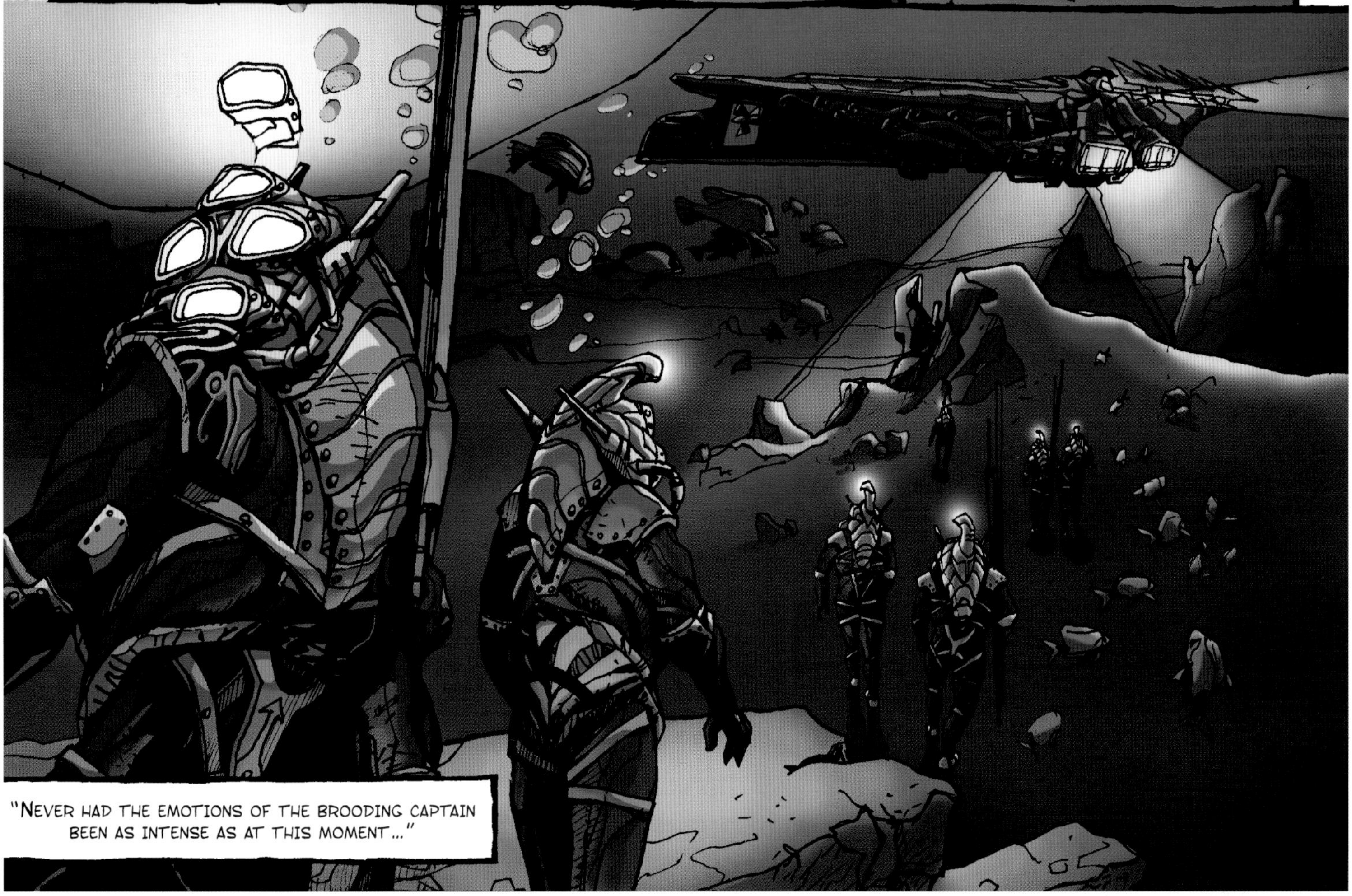
"Never had the emotions of the brooding captain been as intense as at this moment..."

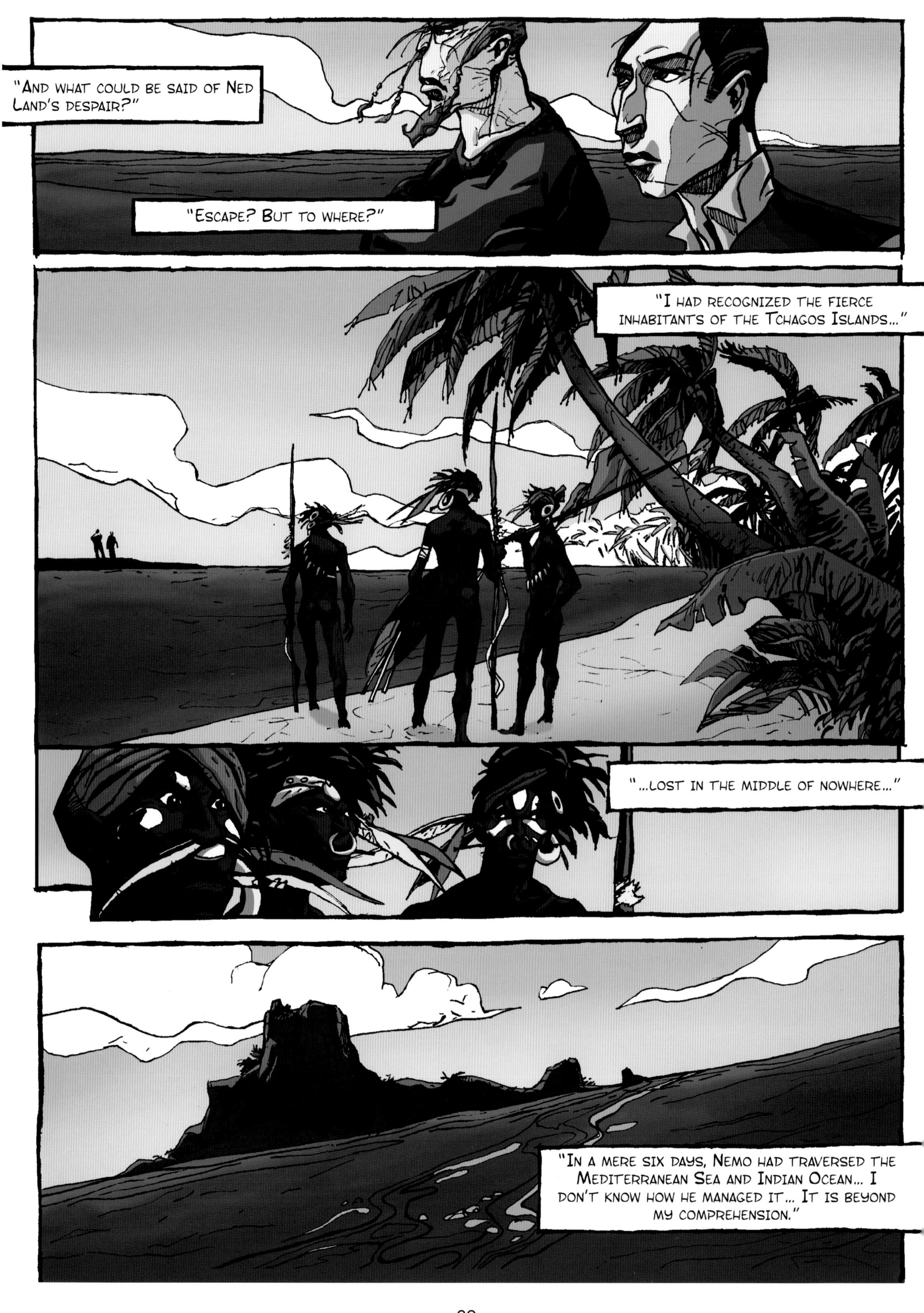
"And what could be said of Ned Land's despair?"
"Escape? But to where?"
"I had recognized the fierce inhabitants of the Tchagos Islands..."
"...lost in the middle of nowhere..."
"In a mere six days, Nemo had traversed the Mediterranean Sea and Indian Ocean... I don't know how he managed it... It is beyond my comprehension."

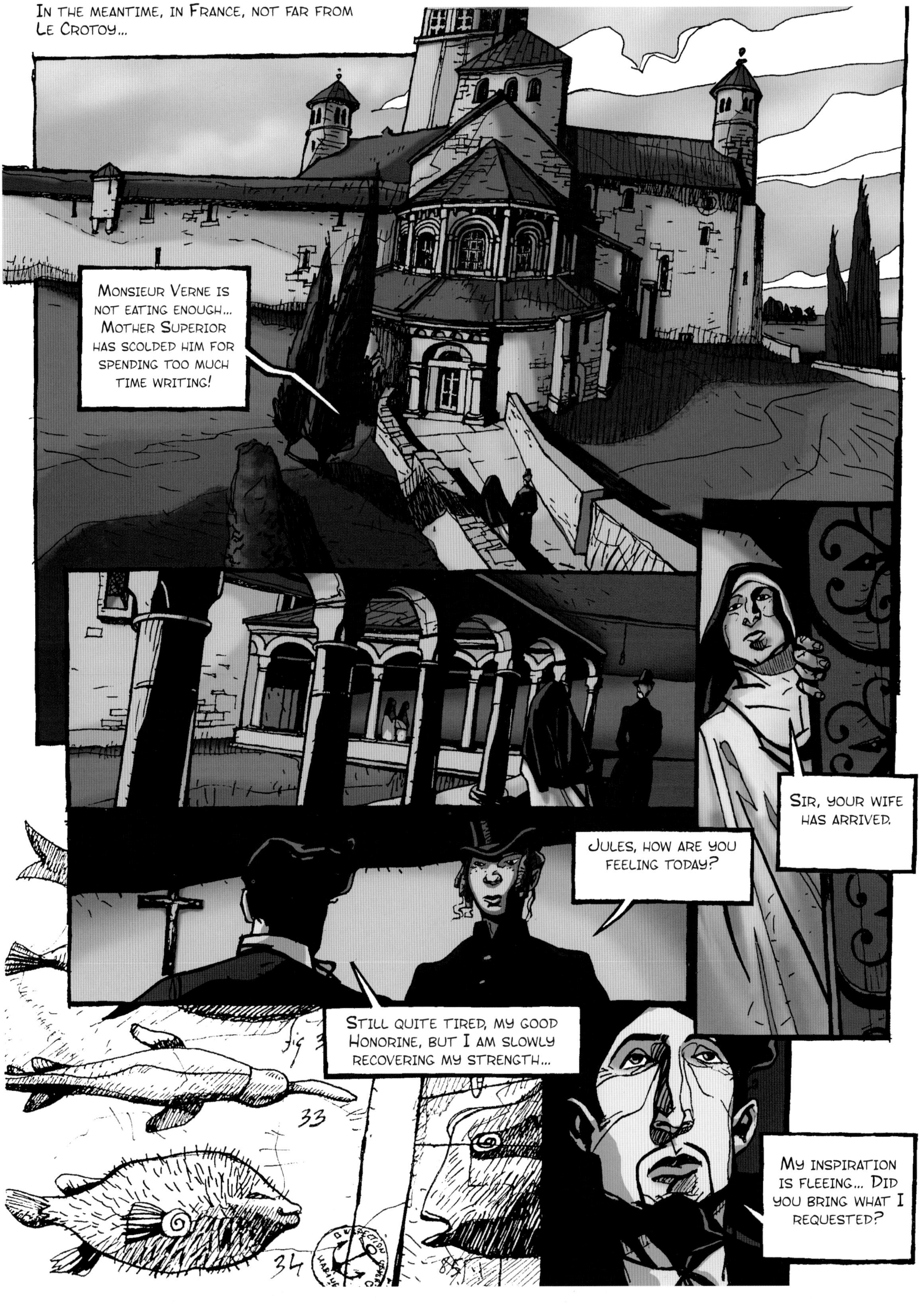
In the meantime, in France, not far from Le Crotoy...
Monsieur Verne is not eating enough... Mother Superior has scolded him for spending too much time writing!
Sir, your wife has arrived.
Jules, how are you feeling today?
Still quite tired, my good Honorine, but I am slowly recovering my strength...
My inspiration is fleeing... Did you bring what I requested?

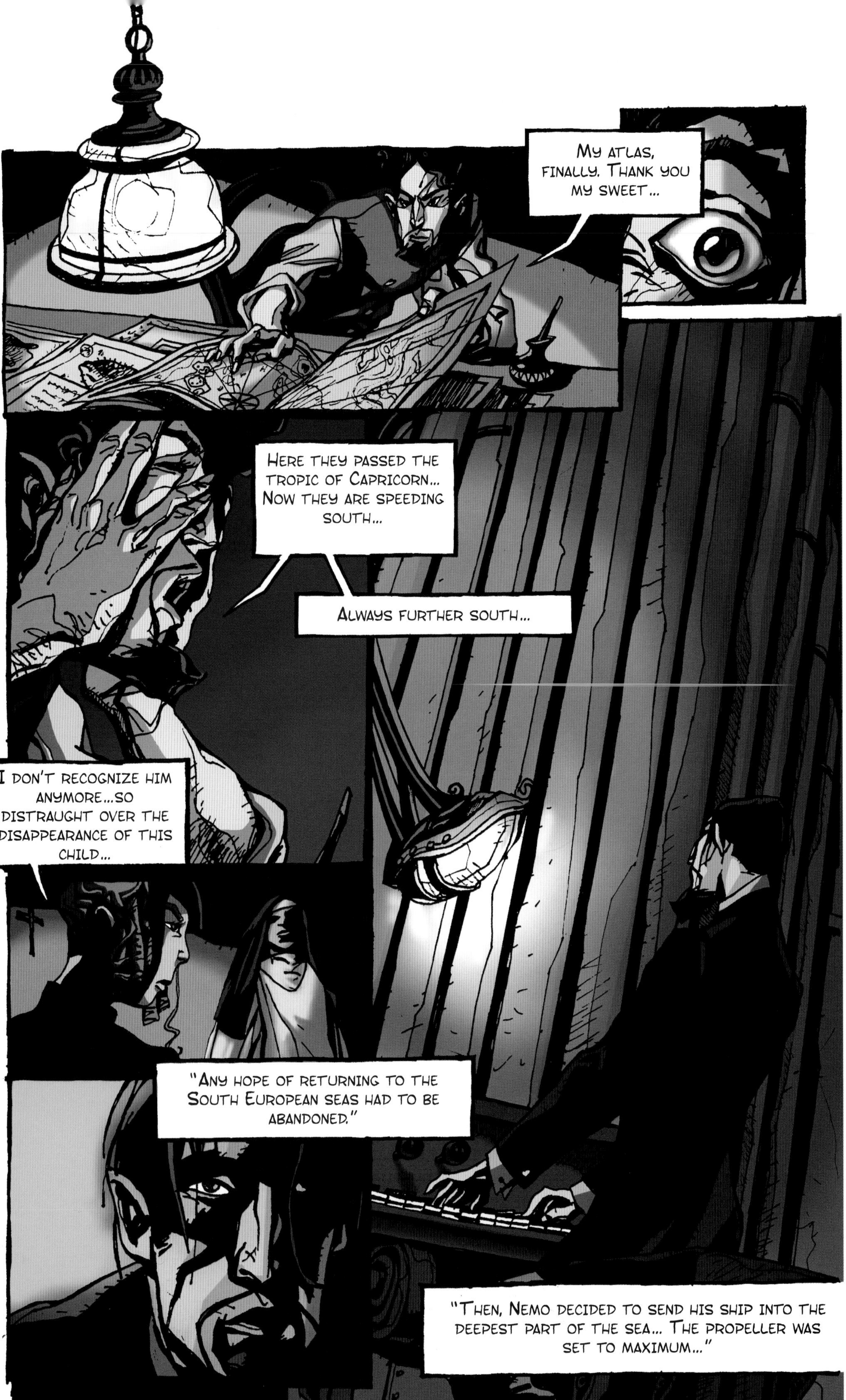
My atlas, finally. Thank you my sweet...
Here they passed the tropic of Capricorn... Now they are speeding south...
Always further south...
I don't recognize him anymore...so distraught over the disappearance of this child...
"Any hope of returning to the South European seas had to be abandoned."
"Then, Nemo decided to send his ship into the deepest part of the sea... The propeller was set to maximum..."

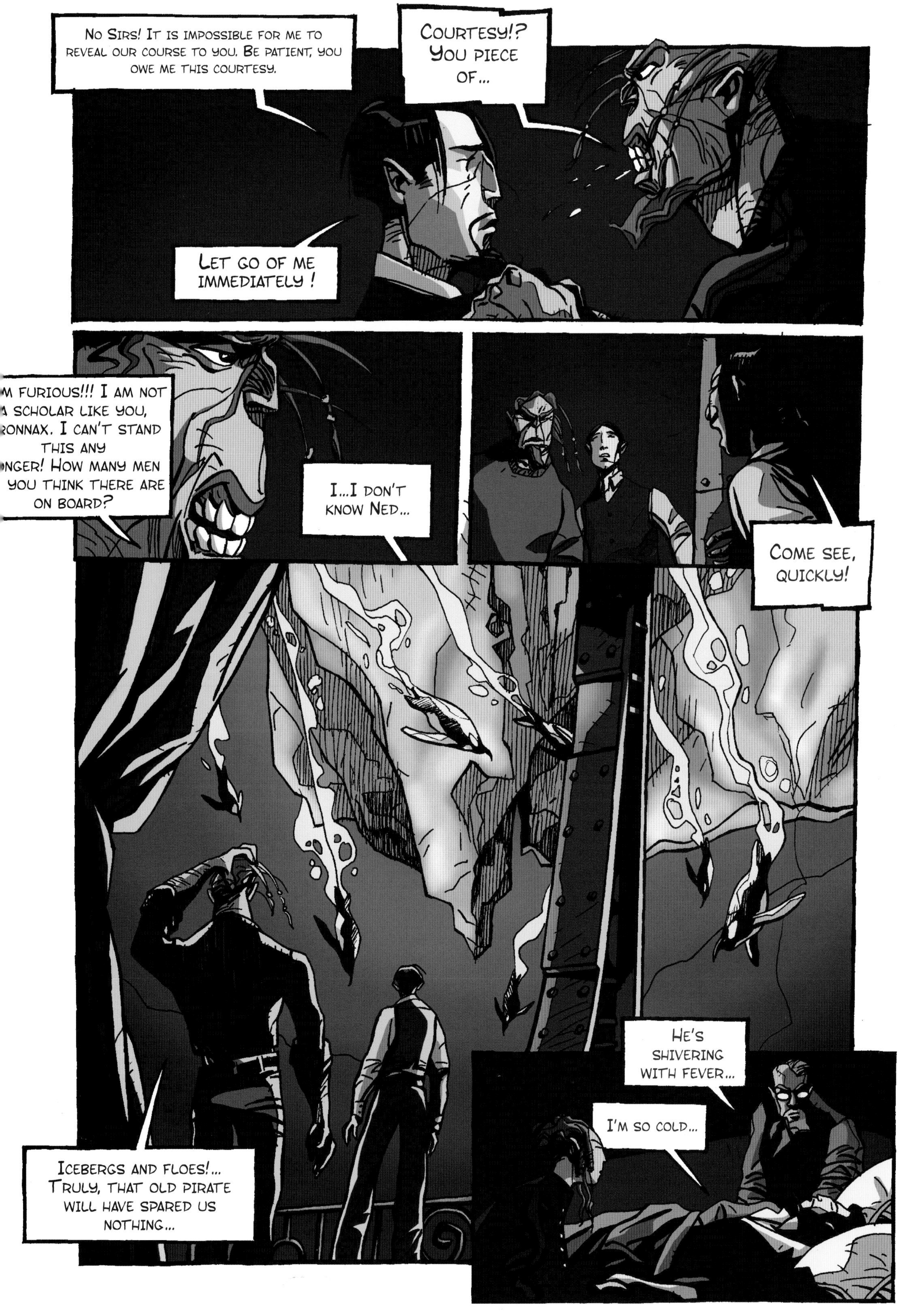
No Sirs! It is impossible for me to reveal our course to you. Be patient, you owe me this courtesy.
Courtesy!? You piece of...
Let go of me immediately !
m furious!!! I am not a scholar like you, ronnax. I can't stand this any nger! How many men you think there are on board?
I...I don't know Ned...
Come see, quickly!
Icebergs and floes!... Truly, that old pirate will have spared us nothing...
He's shivering with fever...
I'm so cold...

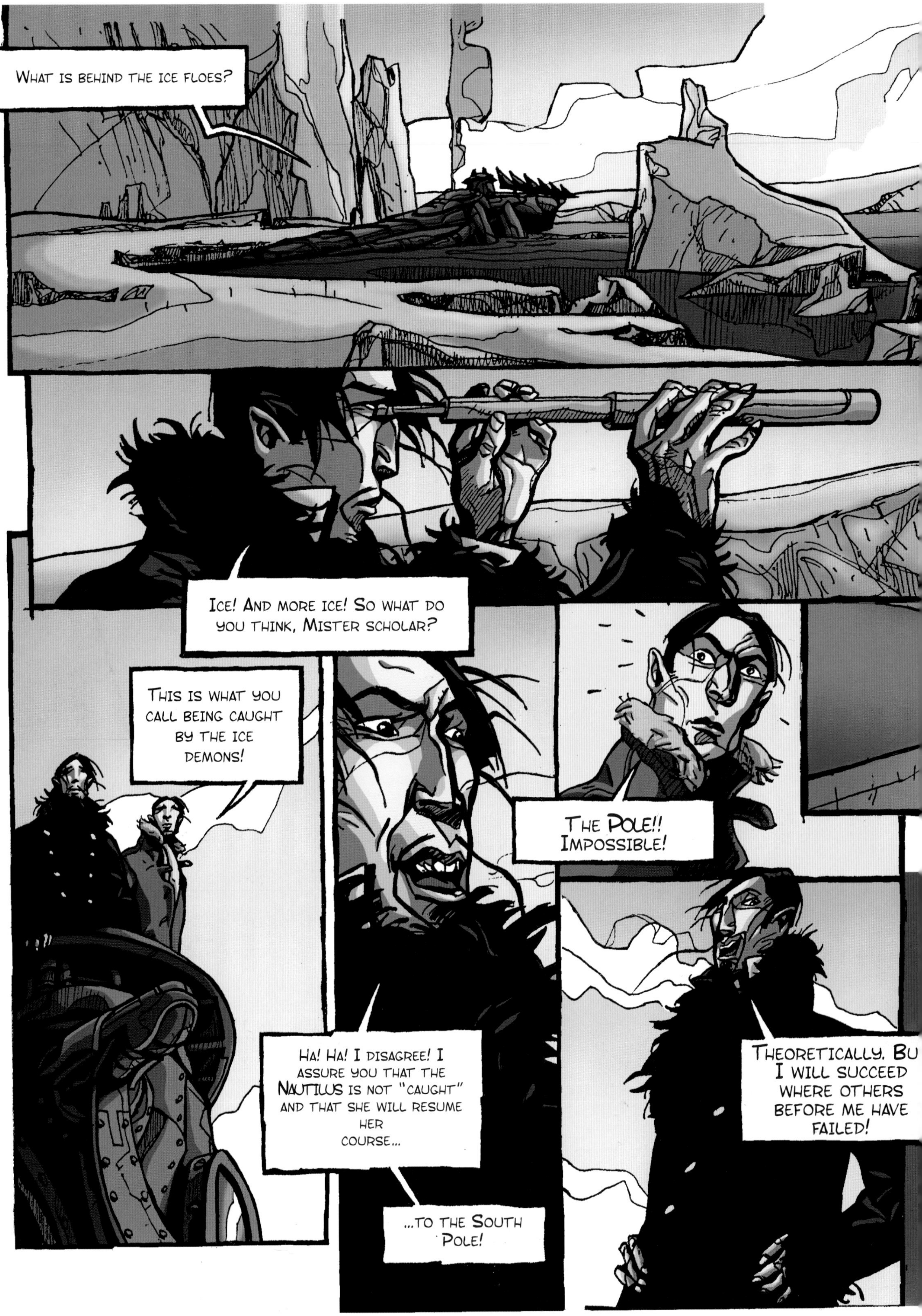
WHAT IS BEHIND THE ICE FLOES?
ICE! AND MORE ICE! SO WHAT DO YOU THINK, MISTER SCHOLAR?
THIS IS WHAT YOU CALL BEING CAUGHT BY THE ICE DEMONS!
HA! HA! I DISAGREE! I ASSURE YOU THAT THE NAUTILUS IS NOT "CAUGHT" AND THAT SHE WILL RESUME HER COURSE...
...TO THE SOUTH POLE!
THE POLE!! IMPOSSIBLE!
THEORETICALLY. BU I WILL SUCCEED WHERE OTHERS BEFORE ME HAVE FAILED!

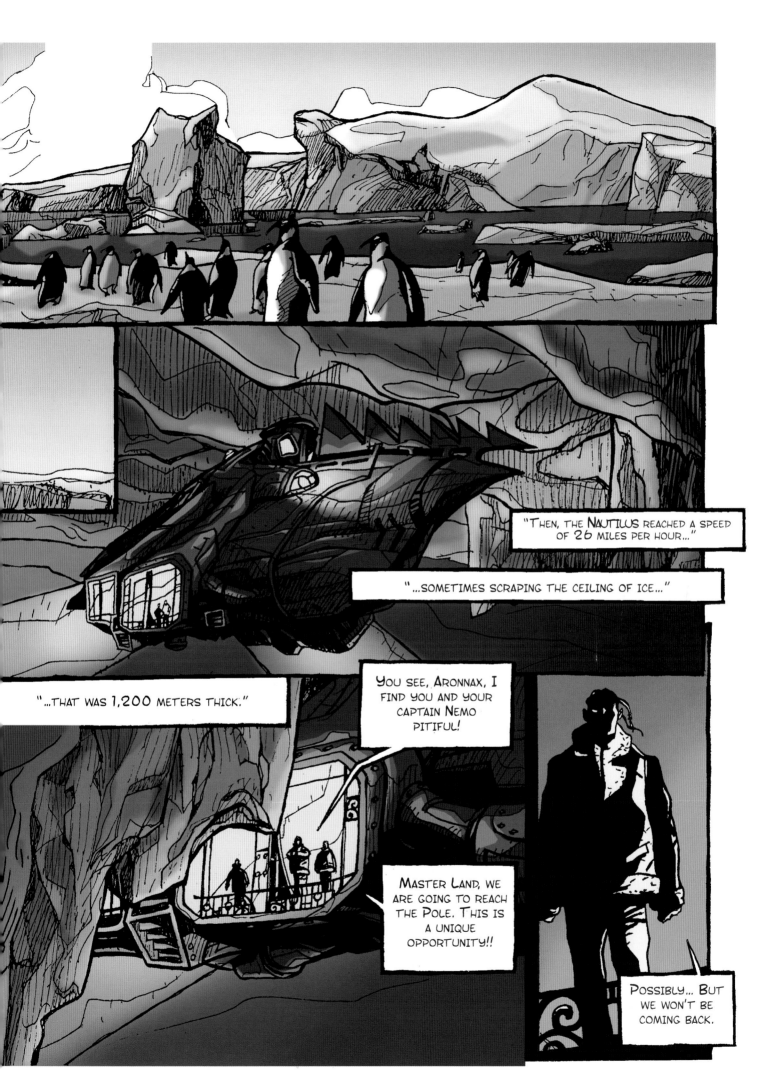

"THEN, THE *NAUTILUS* REACHED A SPEED OF 26 MILES PER HOUR..."

"...SOMETIMES SCRAPING THE CEILING OF ICE..."

"...THAT WAS 1,200 METERS THICK."

YOU SEE, ARONNAX, I FIND YOU AND YOUR CAPTAIN NEMO PITIFUL!

MASTER LAND, WE ARE GOING TO REACH THE POLE. THIS IS A UNIQUE OPPORTUNITY!!

POSSIBLY... BUT WE WON'T BE COMING BACK.

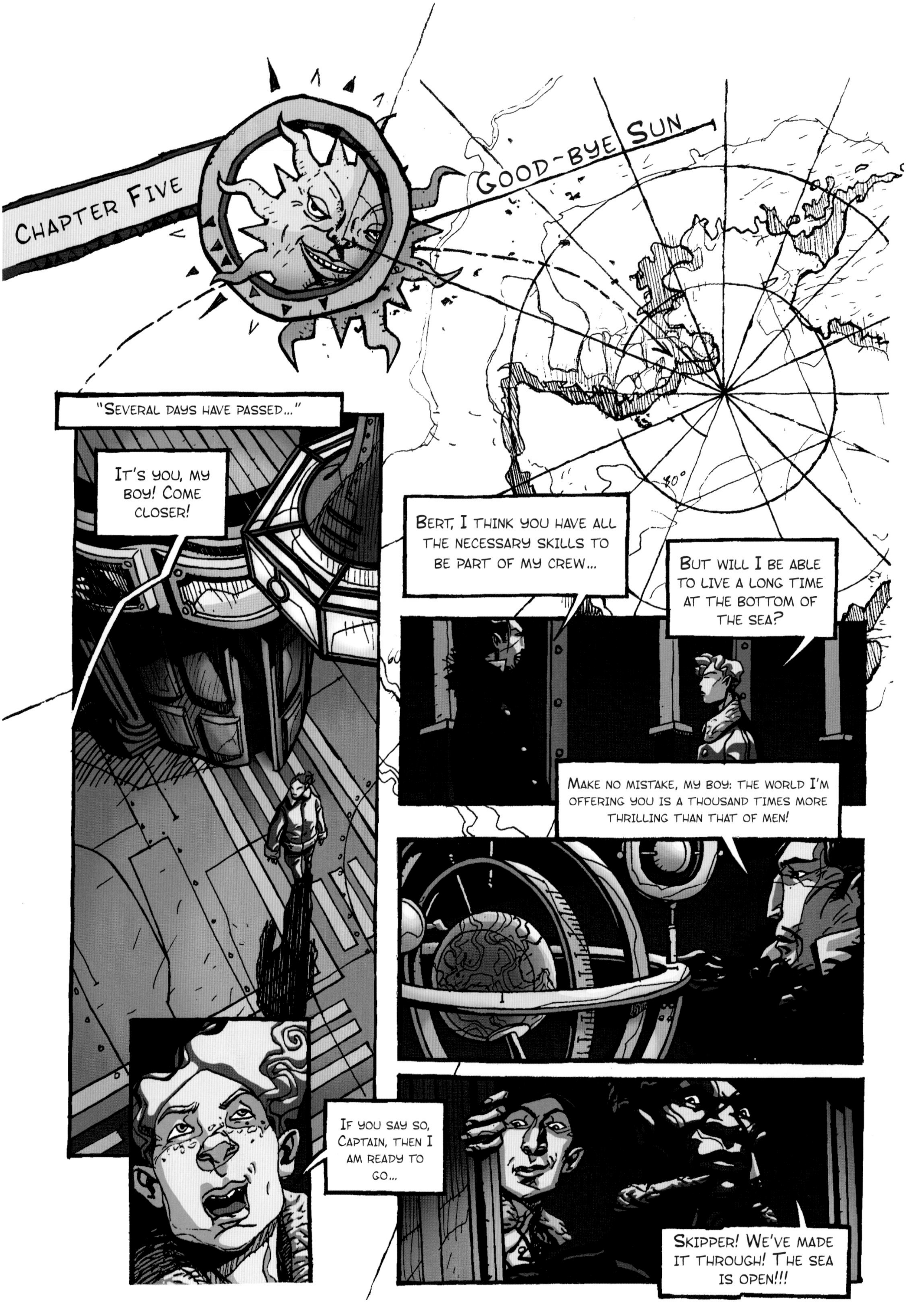
CHAPTER FIVE
GOOD-BYE SUN
"SEVERAL DAYS HAVE PASSED..."
IT'S YOU, MY BOY! COME CLOSER!
BERT, I THINK YOU HAVE ALL THE NECESSARY SKILLS TO BE PART OF MY CREW...
BUT WILL I BE ABLE TO LIVE A LONG TIME AT THE BOTTOM OF THE SEA?
MAKE NO MISTAKE, MY BOY: THE WORLD I'M OFFERING YOU IS A THOUSAND TIMES MORE THRILLING THAN THAT OF MEN!
IF YOU SAY SO, CAPTAIN, THEN I AM READY TO GO...
SKIPPER! WE'VE MADE IT THROUGH! THE SEA IS OPEN!!!

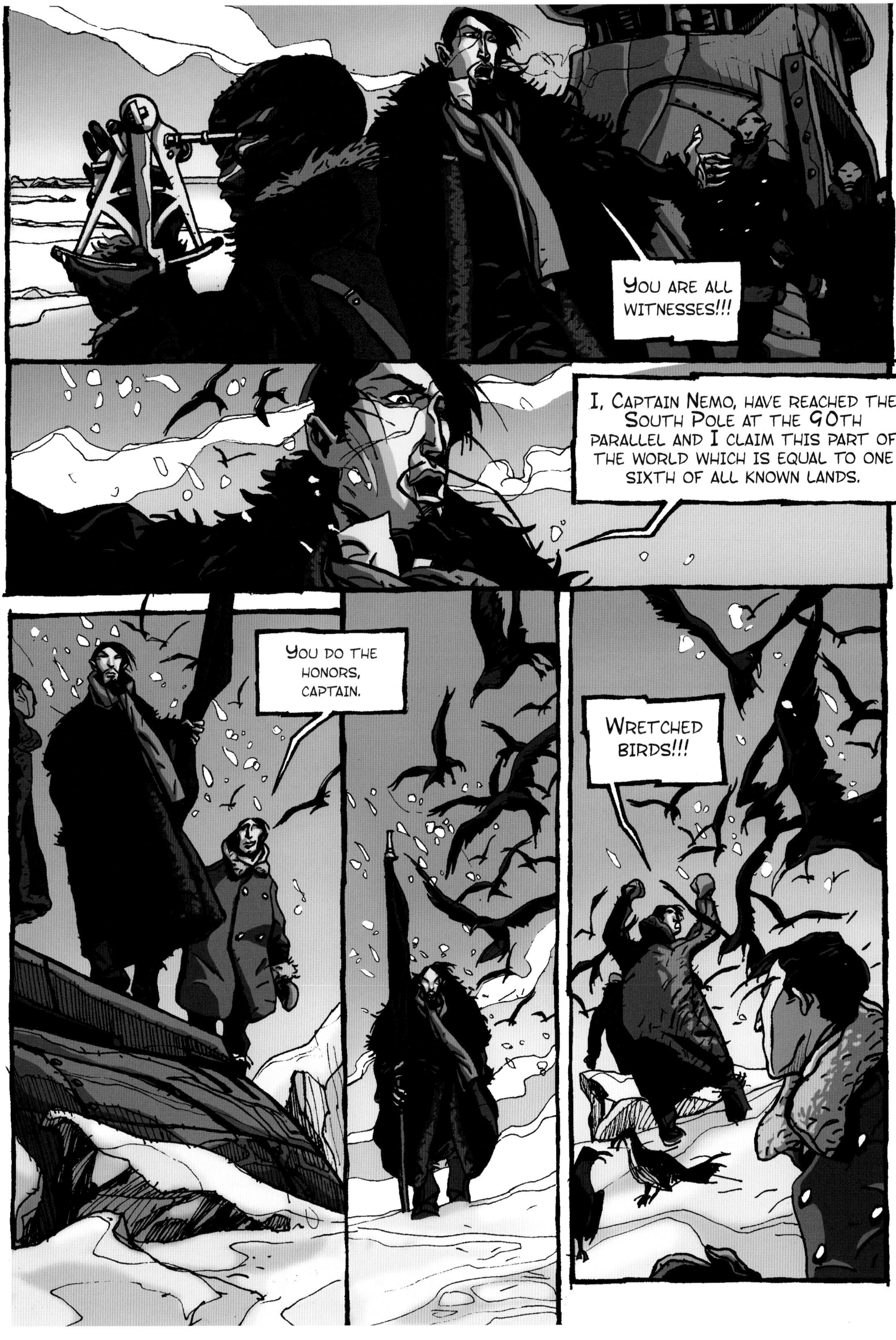

You are all witnesses!!!
I, Captain Nemo, have reached the South Pole at the 90th parallel and I claim this part of the world which is equal to one sixth of all known lands.
You do the honors, captain.
Wretched birds!!!

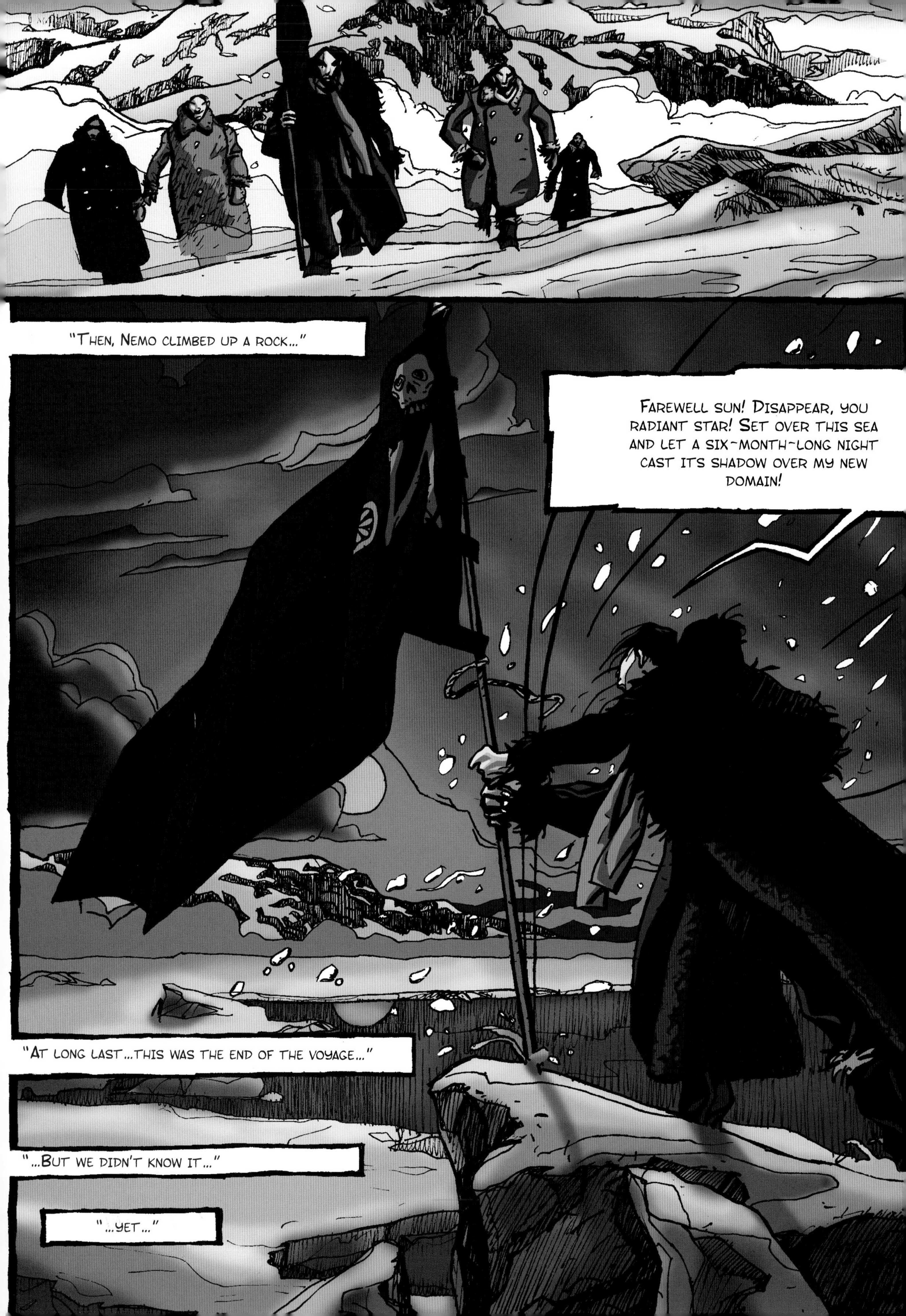
"Then, Nemo climbed up a rock..."
Farewell sun! Disappear, you radiant star! Set over this sea and let a six-month-long night cast its shadow over my new domain!
"At long last...this was the end of the voyage..."
"...But we didn't know it..."
"...yet..."

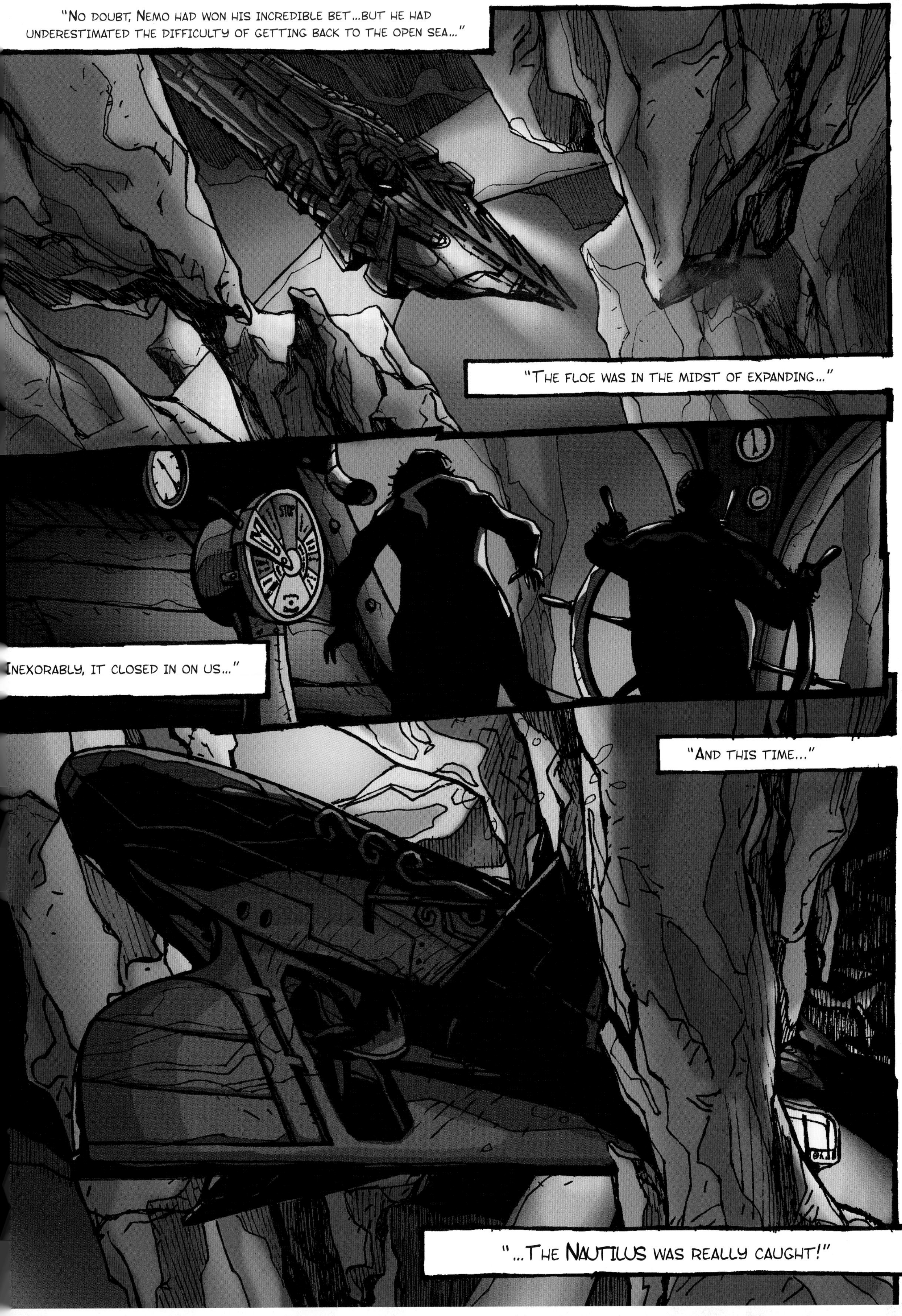
"No doubt, Nemo had won his incredible bet...but he had underestimated the difficulty of getting back to the open sea..."
"The floe was in the midst of expanding..."
STOP
Inexorably, it closed in on us..."
"And this time..."
"...The Nautilus was really caught!"

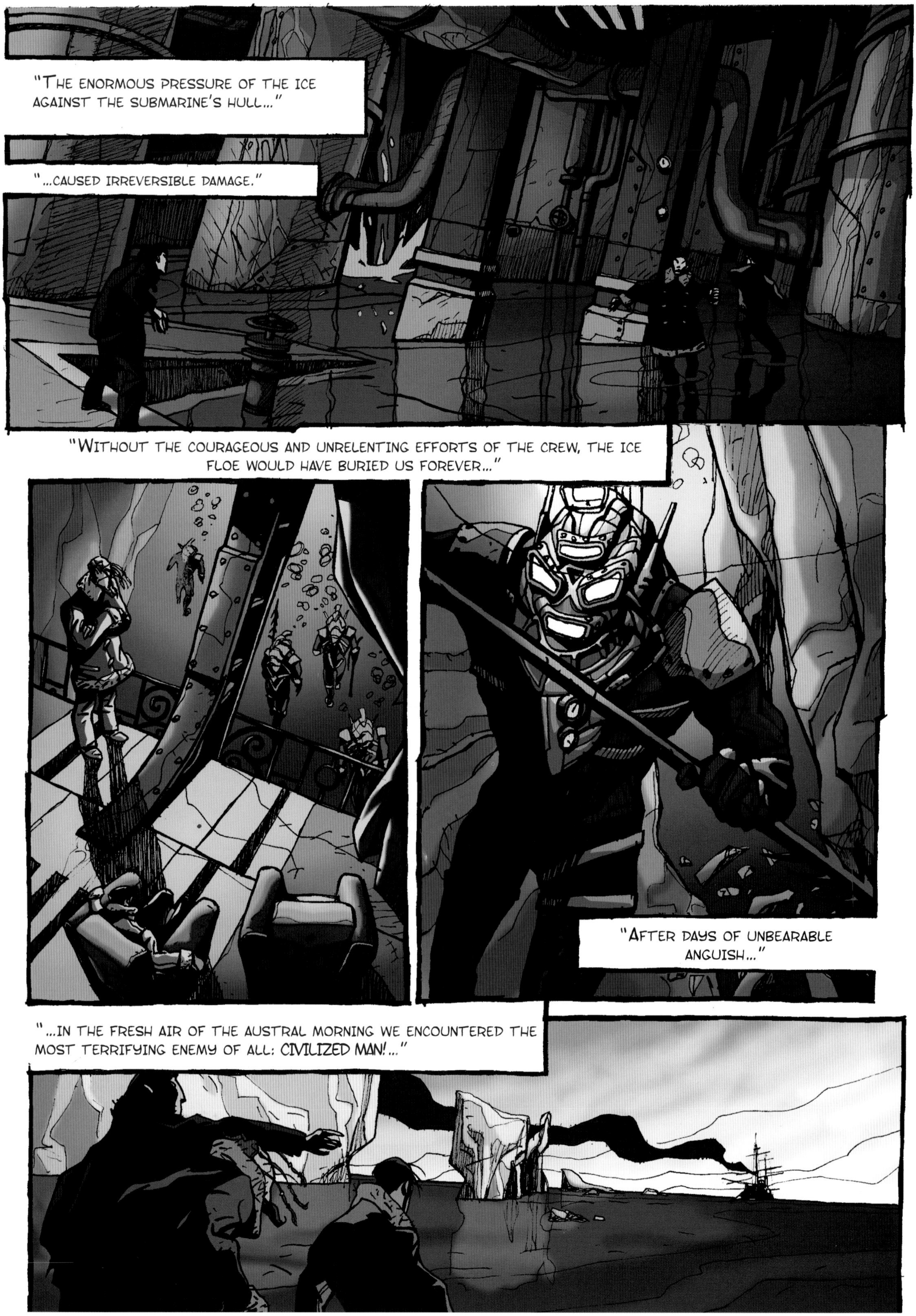
"The enormous pressure of the ice against the submarine's hull..."
"...caused irreversible damage."
"Without the courageous and unrelenting efforts of the crew, the ice floe would have buried us forever..."
"After days of unbearable anguish..."
"...in the fresh air of the austral morning we encountered the most terrifying enemy of all: CIVILIZED MAN!..."

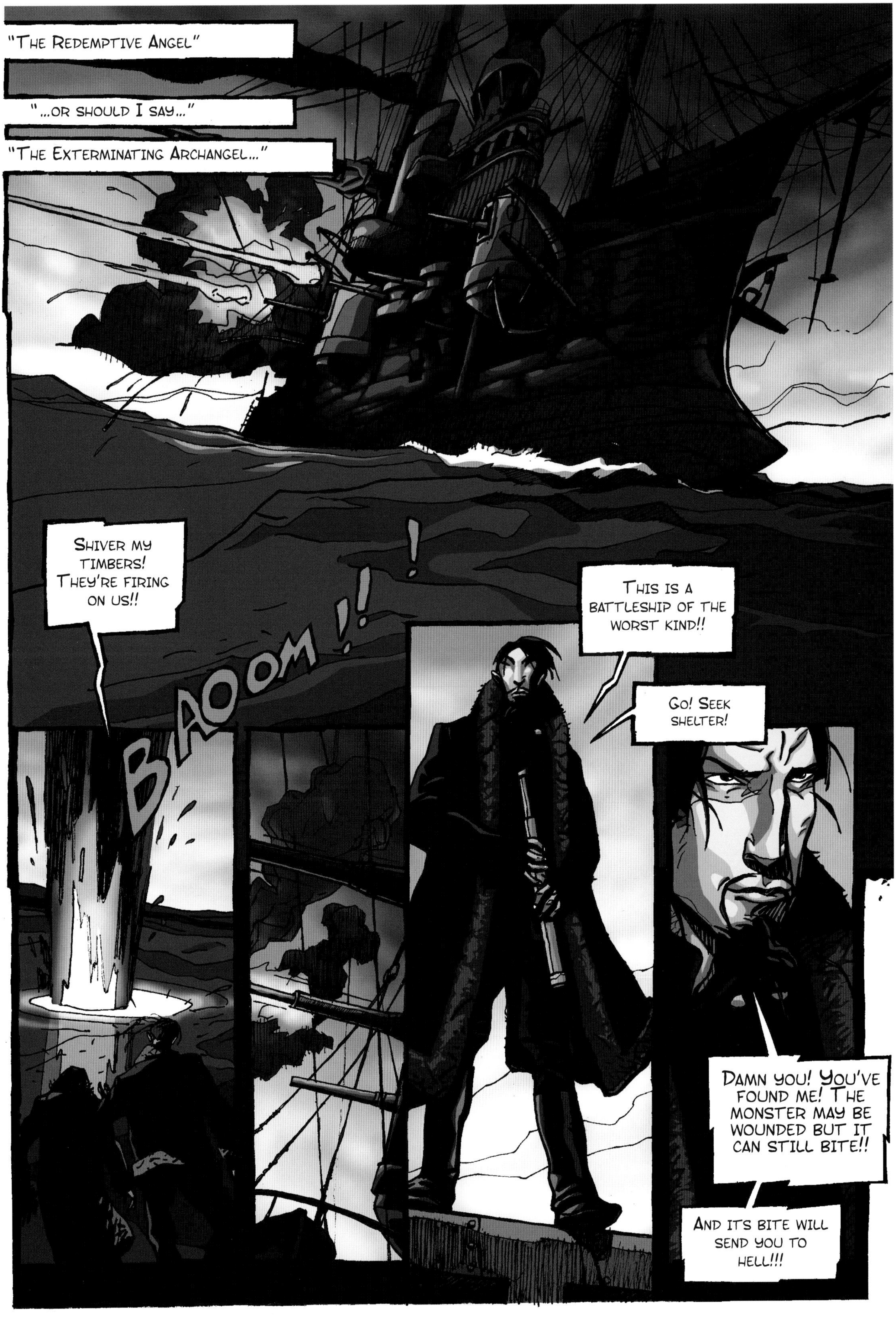
"The Redemptive Angel"
"...or should I say..."
"The Exterminating Archangel..."
Shiver my timbers! They're firing on us!!
!
BAOOM!!
!
This is a battleship of the worst kind!!
Go! Seek shelter!
Damn you! You've found me! The monster may be wounded but it can still bite!!
And its bite will send you to hell!!!

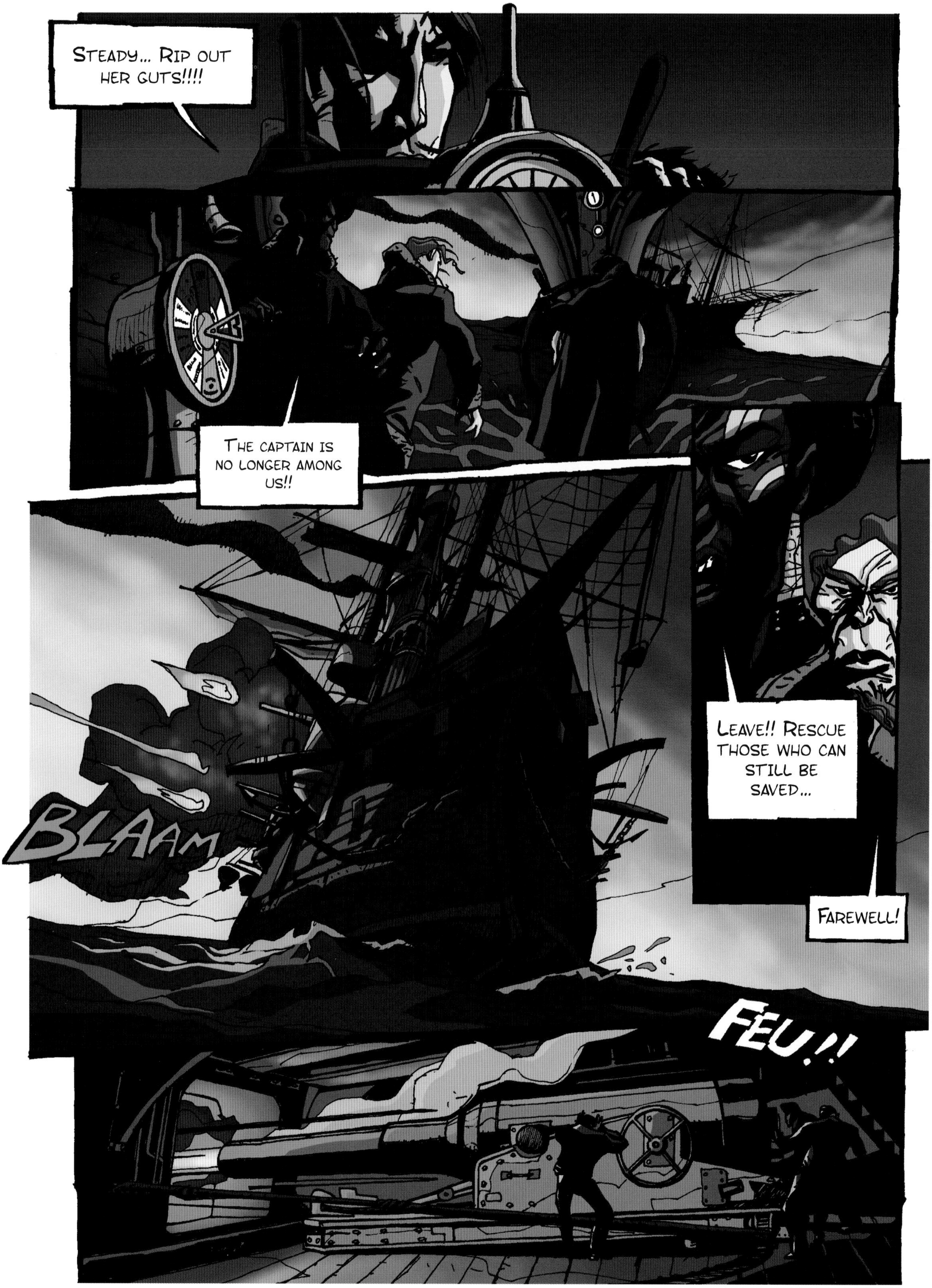
STEADY... RIP OUT HER GUTS!!!!
THE CAPTAIN IS NO LONGER AMONG US!!
BLAAM
LEAVE!! RESCUE THOSE WHO CAN STILL BE SAVED...
FAREWELL!
FEU!!

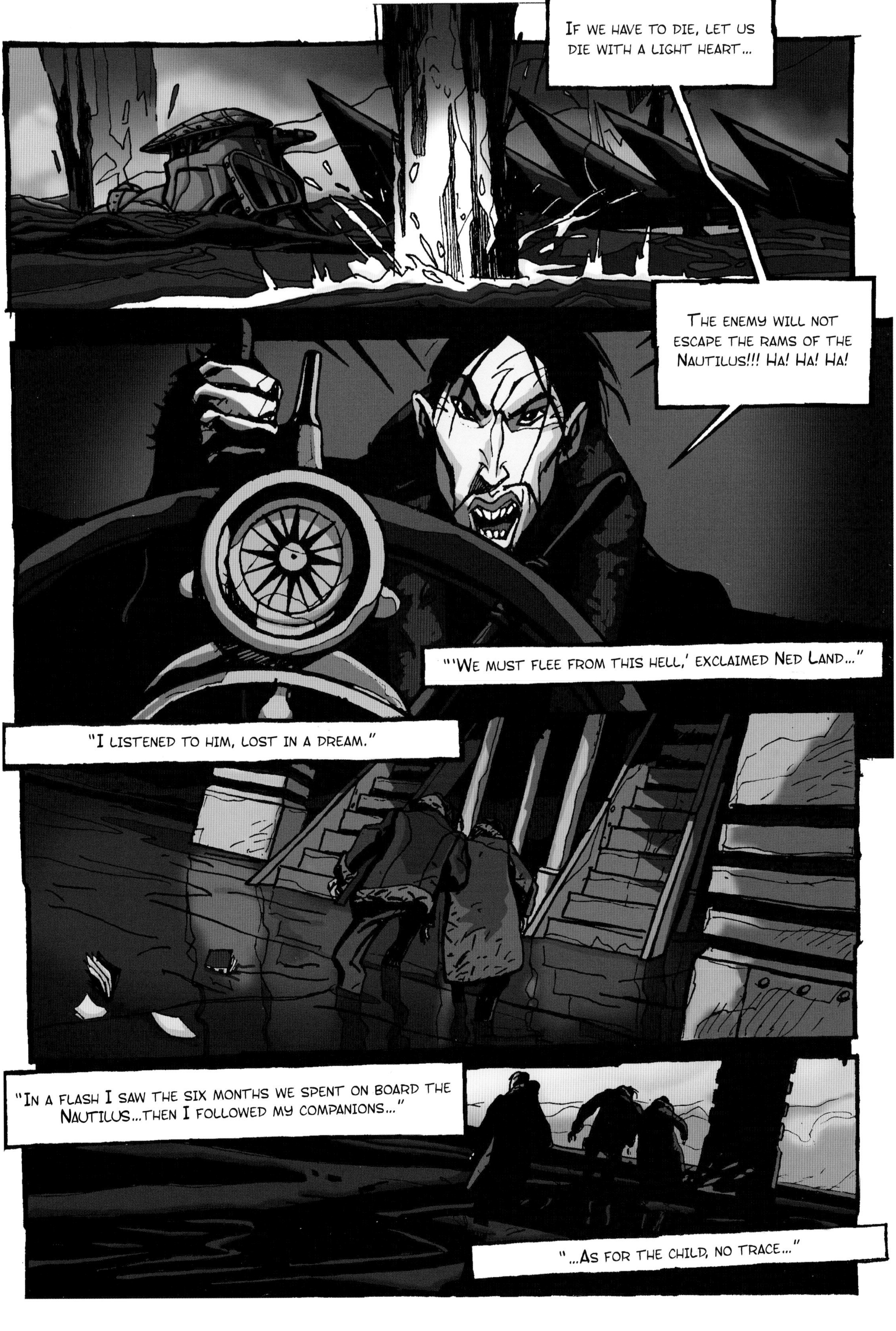
If we have to die, let us die with a light heart...
The enemy will not escape the rams of the Nautilus!!! Ha! Ha! Ha!
"'We must flee from this hell,' exclaimed Ned Land..."
"I listened to him, lost in a dream."
"In a flash I saw the six months we spent on board the Nautilus...then I followed my companions..."
"...As for the child, no trace..."

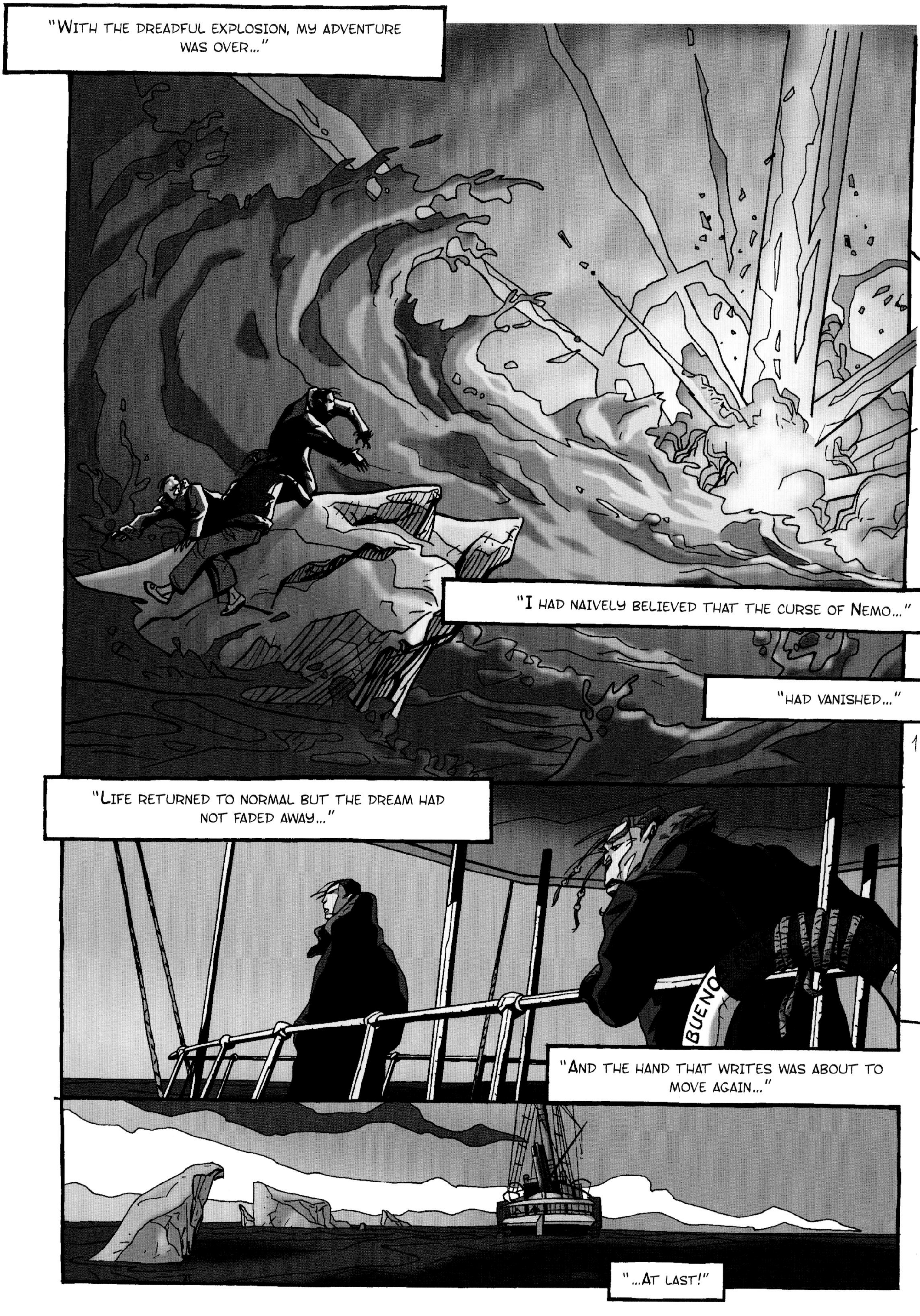
"With the dreadful explosion, my adventure was over..."
"I had naively believed that the curse of Nemo..."
"had vanished..."
"Life returned to normal but the dream had not faded away..."
"And the hand that writes was about to move again..."
"...At last!"

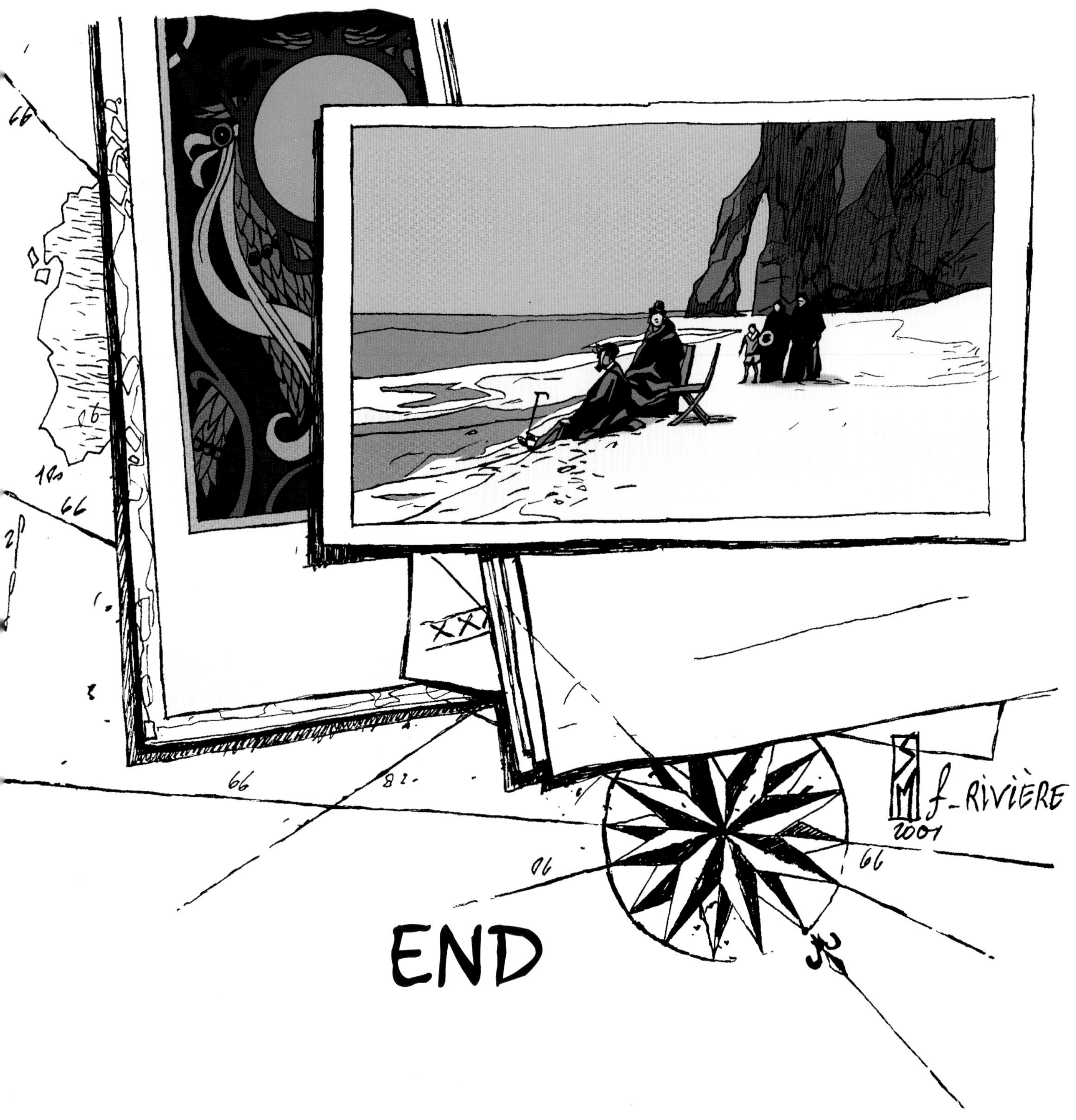
SM f_RIVIÈRE 2001

END

François Rivière, screenwriter, novelist, essayist, and biographer of Frédéric Dard (San Antonio), invested much of himself in the writing of VOYAGE INTO THE DEEP. He remembers the incredible shock he felt upon his first reading of 20,000 LEAGUES UNDER THE SEA. This explains why as an adult he felt it was essential to create an encounter between Nemo, the emblematic fictional character, and Jules Verne, the writer. Taking as its form an "initializing tale," or prequel, leading up to Verne's writing of his masterpiece 20,000 LEAGUES UNDER THE SEA, this account proves to be a passionate homage as much to the author as to the process of literary creation.

Vingt mille lieues sous les mers,

D'après les personnages créés par Jules Verne.

CHAPITRE UN : Le Livre d'eau

"rendre vraisemblable ce qui est invraisemblable..."

PLANCHE I

Le Crotoy, dans la Somme, un soir de 1868

a. Une silhouette courbée marche en direction d'un phare (éteint) sur un promontoire dominant la mer. Une nuit sans lune.
b. La silhouette pénêtre dans la tour du phare.
c. On s'aperçoit q'un enfant d'une douzaine d'années (mais on ne tingue que sa mince silhouette encapuchonnée, qui le rend asex a suivi l'homme et s'avance à présent lui aussi vers le phare.
d. L'homme, dans l'escalier à vis, arrive au sommet du phare.
e. Il enclenche le mécanisme qui allume l'énorme lanterne - son barbu est éclairé en lumière rasante : c'est Jules Verne.
f. Le phare émet un puissant faisceau qui éclaire la mer sur une longue distance

PLANCHE 2

a. L'enfant fasciné (il est arrivé au sommet et se tient derriè qui ne l'a pas encore vu) met une main en visière pour observe lueur du phare.

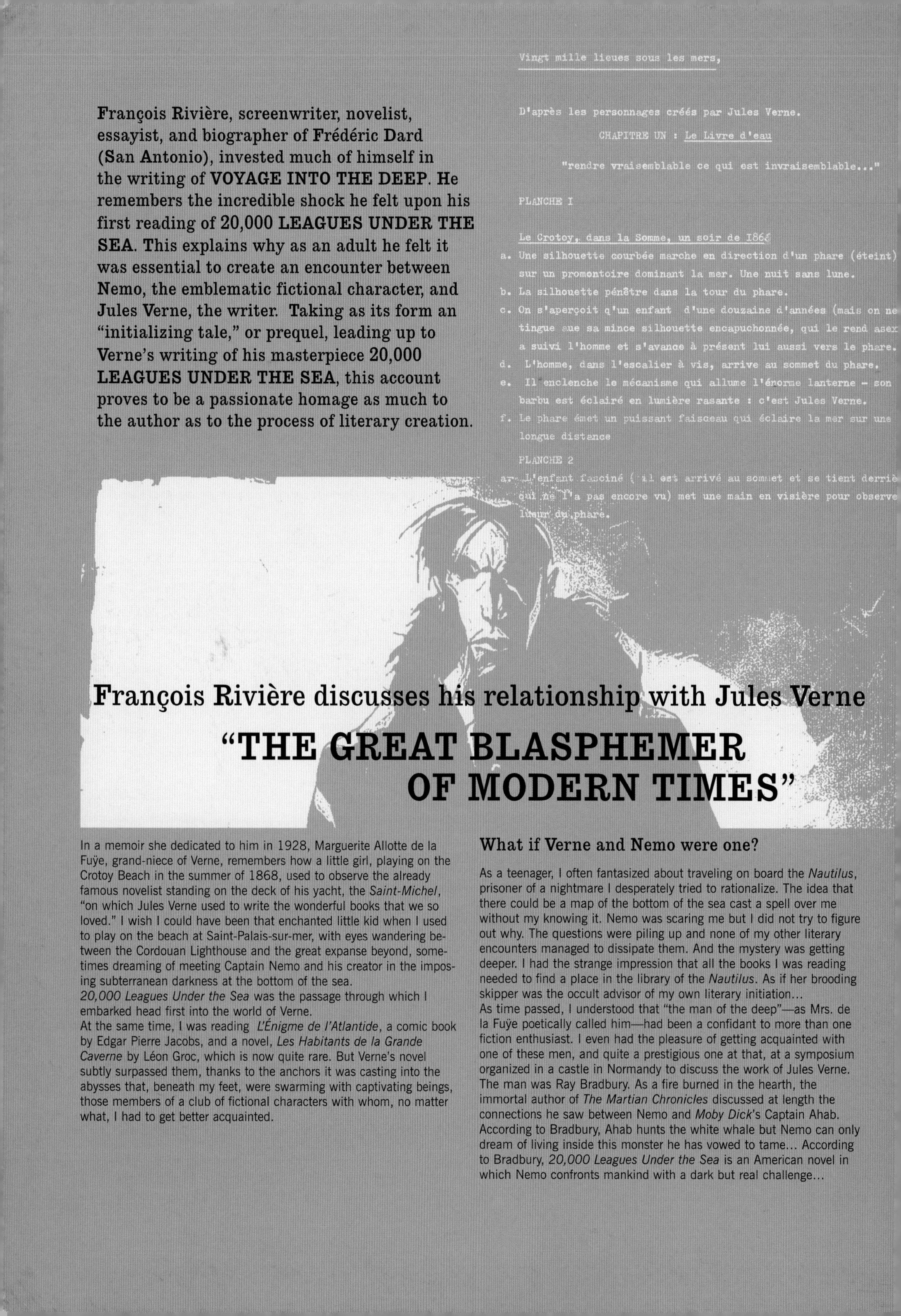

François Rivière discusses his relationship with Jules Verne

"THE GREAT BLASPHEMER OF MODERN TIMES"

In a memoir she dedicated to him in 1928, Marguerite Allotte de la Fuÿe, grand-niece of Verne, remembers how a little girl, playing on the Crotoy Beach in the summer of 1868, used to observe the already famous novelist standing on the deck of his yacht, the *Saint-Michel*, "on which Jules Verne used to write the wonderful books that we so loved." I wish I could have been that enchanted little kid when I used to play on the beach at Saint-Palais-sur-mer, with eyes wandering between the Cordouan Lighthouse and the great expanse beyond, sometimes dreaming of meeting Captain Nemo and his creator in the imposing subterranean darkness at the bottom of the sea.

20,000 Leagues Under the Sea was the passage through which I embarked head first into the world of Verne.

At the same time, I was reading *L'Énigme de l'Atlantide*, a comic book by Edgar Pierre Jacobs, and a novel, *Les Habitants de la Grande Caverne* by Léon Groc, which is now quite rare. But Verne's novel subtly surpassed them, thanks to the anchors it was casting into the abysses that, beneath my feet, were swarming with captivating beings, those members of a club of fictional characters with whom, no matter what, I had to get better acquainted.

What if Verne and Nemo were one?

As a teenager, I often fantasized about traveling on board the *Nautilus*, prisoner of a nightmare I desperately tried to rationalize. The idea that there could be a map of the bottom of the sea cast a spell over me without my knowing it. Nemo was scaring me but I did not try to figure out why. The questions were piling up and none of my other literary encounters managed to dissipate them. And the mystery was getting deeper. I had the strange impression that all the books I was reading needed to find a place in the library of the *Nautilus*. As if her brooding skipper was the occult advisor of my own literary initiation...

As time passed, I understood that "the man of the deep"—as Mrs. de la Fuÿe poetically called him—had been a confidant to more than one fiction enthusiast. I even had the pleasure of getting acquainted with one of these men, and quite a prestigious one at that, at a symposium organized in a castle in Normandy to discuss the work of Jules Verne. The man was Ray Bradbury. As a fire burned in the hearth, the immortal author of *The Martian Chronicles* discussed at length the connections he saw between Nemo and *Moby Dick*'s Captain Ahab. According to Bradbury, Ahab hunts the white whale but Nemo can only dream of living inside this monster he has vowed to tame... According to Bradbury, *20,000 Leagues Under the Sea* is an American novel in which Nemo confronts mankind with a dark but real challenge...

I wished I could have received a posthumous letter from Jules Verne, but could I not appropriately assume that Ray Bradbury had been his interpreter? I met with the American novelist again on several occasions, one of which was when he whimsically came and spent the month of July in Paris incognito, dawdling along in the streets that felt to him like a giant setting from his favorite movie, *The Hunchback of Notre-Dame.*

Each time we met, I told him how helpless I felt about the lack of interest shown by official French cultural institutions toward the man he had once called "the greatest blasphemer of modern times." And Ray Bradbury could only agree with me, as the Anglo-Saxons, the Italians, and not a few readers from Eastern Europe have always stood in awe of Jules Verne and his creations. But this has never happened in France.

Jules Verne, sans se retourner - expression navrée, fatiguée :
" Encore cette voix d'enfant...Elle me poursuivra donc toujours ?"
.'enfant s'avance - il a ôté son capuchon et offre l'apparence d'un
eune garçon - et se tourne vers le romancier, à présent étonné.
" - Que fais-tu ici, petit ? Tu devrais être couché."
" - Je suis venu voir le navire sous-marin...Cela ne vous dérange
pas, j'espère ?"
ros plan du visage de Verne, sourcils fronçés :
' - De quoi parles-tu ?"
Le garçonnet : " Il n'a pas de nom...Son capitaine non plus n'a pas
de nom..."

MOBILIS IN MOBIL
N

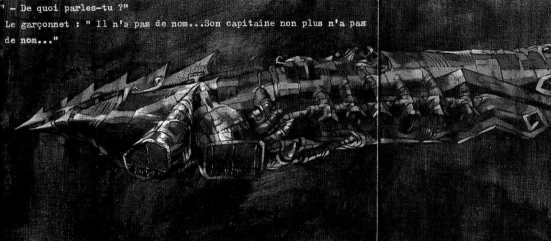

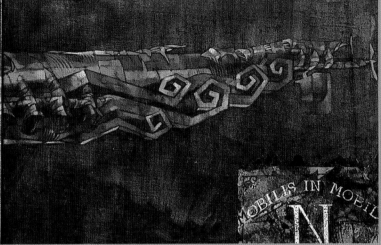

"According to science-fiction writer Ray Bradbury, 20,000 LEAGUES UNDER THE SEA is an American novel."

I reread Verne's work, trying to read between the lines. But I only succeeded in getting intoxicated with the music of the words, with their magic... This is when a face suddenly appeared at one of the submarine's portholes: it was Raymond Roussel, the genuine poet and eccentric millionaire who said that his books, published at his own expense at the beginning of the twentieth century, were born out of the same processes as Verne's novels. I devoured Roussel's books—*Impressions of Africa, Locus Solus*—basking in the words he wrote about my idol: "I would like, in this note, to pay tribute to the man of immeasurable genius, Jules Verne. The admiration I have for him is boundless. I had the joy of being welcomed by him in Amiens, where I was doing my military service, and was allowed to shake the hand that had written so many immortal works. Oh, incomparable master, may the Lord bless you for all these sublime hours I spent reading and rereading you over and over again." The young Roussel had read into Jules Verne as if he was reading coffee dregs, and his ecstasy was close to that of a visionary.

The tribute that became the journey

Several years later, with the collaboration of the illustrator Andreas, I created a reverent homage to both Verne and his admirer in the form of a comic strip entitled "La Visitation d'Amiens,"[1] later published in the collection *Révélations Posthumes*.[2] I came up with the idea of allowing my literary envy to be poured into short stories that would feature the authors who had been haunting me for some time: H. P. Lovecraft, Agatha Christie, Pierre Loti. I included a painter, the genius Paul Delvaux, who was generous enough to read the outrageous anecdote devoted to him and speak kindly of it...

[1] "The Amiens Visitation"
[2] *Posthumous Revelations*

The discovery of a power: reading the unreadable

Throughout the years, I maintained a very romantic idea of this author whose characters remained completely inseparable from his creation. I believe that Jules Verne's adventures were those of a genuine pioneer of modern fiction. Especially in regards to what British science-fiction writers—here I am thinking of Michael Moorcock or J. G. Ballard—call "speculative fiction." In the early seventies, one of these writers, Ian Watson, dropped a bombshell over the sea of the imagination of the previous century: his novel *The Embedding* very likely managed what dear Raymond Roussel, caught up in the insane demands of his own high poetic standards, could not. Watson's book relayed the reality of a mental state that, obtained through the ingestion of hallucinatory substances, enabled reading into the unreadable—that is, moving freely through Verne's and Roussel's processes!

Of course, a small tribe of science-fiction enthusiasts duly celebrated Watson's revelation. As was to be expected, none of the official culture gurus cared. And yet, this would have been a beautiful opportunity to pay homage to Verne's modernity. For a brief period of time, a few academic speculators working at the frontiers of Pataphysics made a point to compile Verne's puns, but never bothered to venture any further. Then once again, silence.

An immortal human being, a fascinating writer

One day, some forgotten manuscripts of the great writer resurfaced. This must have caused some grief to my dear friend Luce Courville who in 1978, the year of the 150th anniversary of Verne's birth, started the Jules Verne museum in Nantes. And there was yet another discovery: from an abandoned trunk, Jules's own great-grandson found a novel which had been rejected by Hetzel, his publisher: *Paris in the Twentieth Century*. Avenged, at last, from editorial censorship—that he himself equated to unfair paternal punishment—Verne made a brief comeback as his lost-and-then-found book became an international best-seller...

A DRAMA IN LIVONIA begins the Vernian exploration

The idea of paying another tribute to the ancestor of all of my readerly delights was still on my mind—a chance encounter was the sign to begin again. Serge Micheli, a young Corsican illustrator, confided in me that ever since his childhood he had been living in awe of the author of *20,000 Leagues Under the Sea*. Obsessively haunted by Nemo, he dreamed of giving him a face... Our first gallop was with *A Drama in Livonia*, an underrated and politically engaged detective story by Jules Verne that we adapted two years ago. Now, the stakes have taken on a different nature: Captain Nemo and Jules Verne blended into one.
I once again read Marguerite Allotte de la Fuÿe's book, and again felt the strength of her passion for "the man who no longer wants a name, the Nobody of classical poetry, the fugitive from the earth who, once dead, will rest with a few chosen comrades in the coral cemetery."

I also found these words from one of Verne's nephews who often sailed with the novelist on the *Saint-Michel*: "In fact, my uncle Jules only ever had three passions: freedom, music and the sea."
Freedom and the sea, but above all some kind of demiurgic madness—was what Serge Micheli and I felt should be given paramount importance in the narrative we imagined. This madness has been our music, a music that, played on the organ of the *Nautilus*, can be heard over the roar of waves. But the true soundtrack of *Voyage Into the Deep*—Verne's working title for the novel—is the haunting whisper of creation... What turns Jules Verne into a wizard and exposes him to the dangerous rhythm of visions, and of encounters... Verne, soon to lose his grip on the real world, becomes a character in his own fiction and drags some of the people surrounding him into it... Verne, whose personality splits and who becomes, under the alias of Nemo, the picture of his own interior existence.

Return to Le Crotoy

At the end of the spring of 1868, Jules Verne wrote to his father: "I am writing you from Dieppe, where the winds lead me in the *Saint-Michel*. You can send your reply to Le Crotoy, where I will return as soon as the sea will allow for it. It is very agitated at the moment and prevents us, the skipper and I, from going out. But as the *Saint-Michel* is a floating library, I can work here better than on dry land. I will soon complete the first volume of *20,000 Leagues Under the Sea*, and hope that all these implausibilities will seem plausible."
The implausibilities of this fantastic novel have become legendary, and on both hemispheres it is all the little boys who made it the stuff of their childhood reveries who have become the intrepid heroes of *Voyage into the Deep*... Serge Micheli and I renounce nothing of our youths; we still share the same desire to bring the colors and the sounds back to life, to celebrate now and forever the mysterious longing pervading the adventures of Captain Nemo and his companions... On the beach of Le Crotoy, upon which the hypnotic moon of Paul Delvaux's paintings casts its light, a little girl is running toward the outline of the yacht... She has grown up and has taken the oriental charm of our heroine... The young princess runs on the sands of fiction's past, present and future, searching for her father.

—François Rivière
May 2002

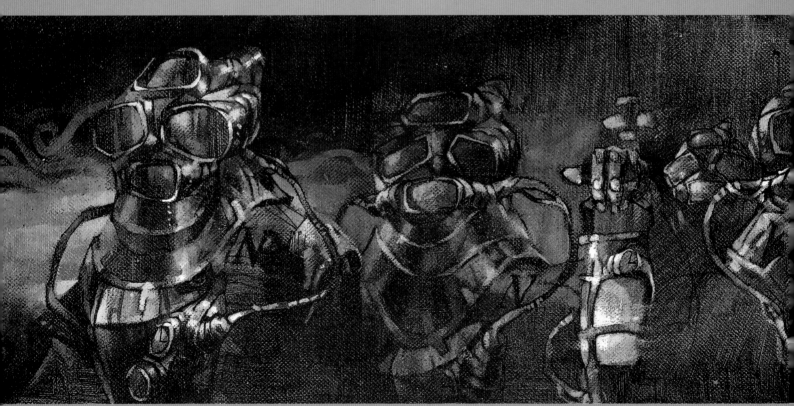

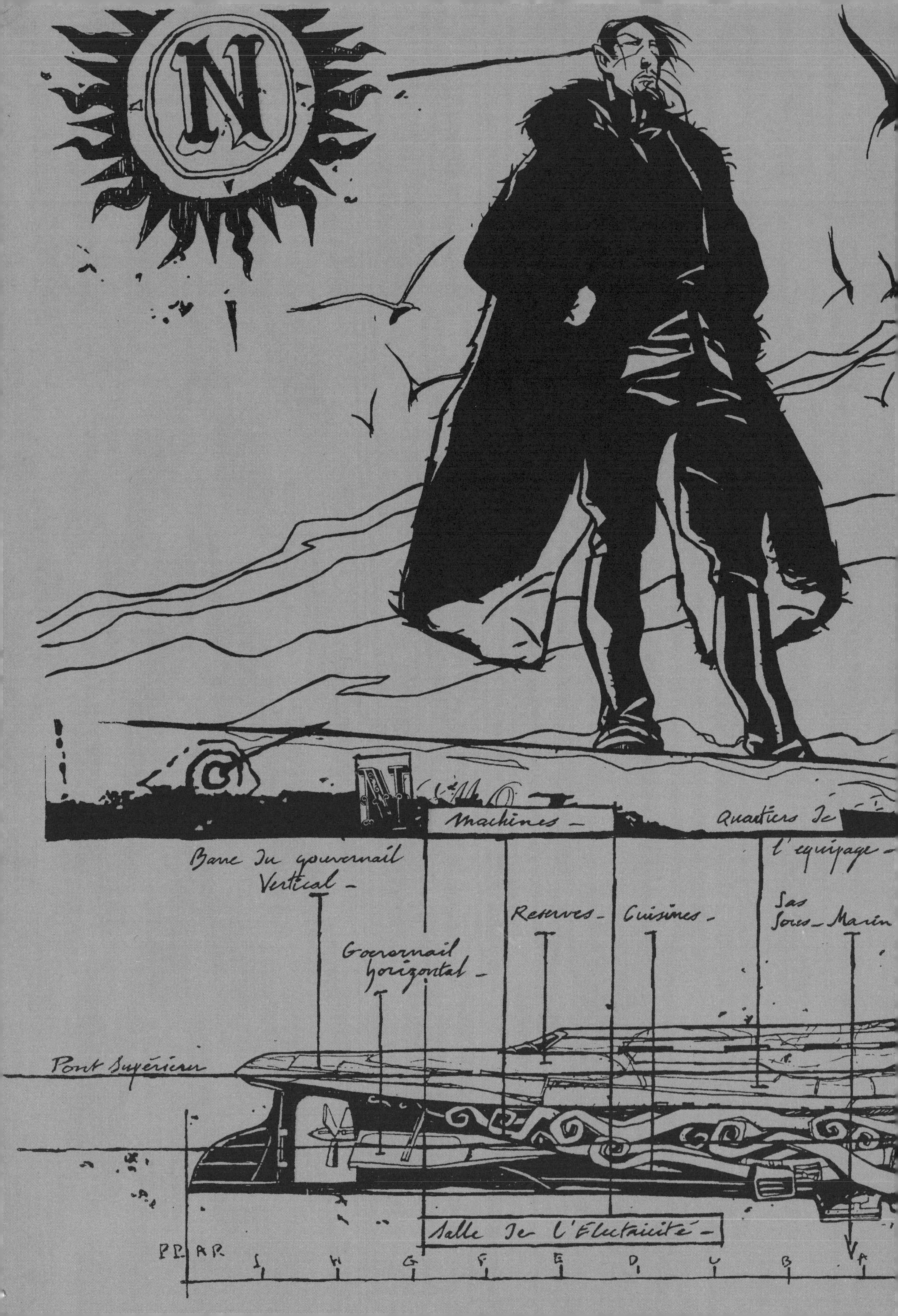
N
Machines -
Quartiers de l'équipage -
Barre du gouvernail Vertical -
Reserves -
Cuisines -
Sas Sous-Marin
Gouvernail horizontal -
Pont Supérieur
Salle de l'Electricité -
PP. AP. I H G F E D C B A